Fiction to look ou
The Obse....

Books to watch out for in 2021
Irish Times

'Fuks's skill lies in his quiet exploration of how exclusion – willed or imposed – shapes experience within families.' —*The New York Times*

'A brilliant achievement.' —*Le Monde*

'Fuks impressively inhabits the near despair that comes with the fragmentation of family and country.' —*Kirkus*

'Fuk's work, while challenging in form, comes together in a powerful way.' —*Publishers Weekly*

'Fuks' writing is sharp and humane, intimate and lyrical.' —*Mark Haber, Brazos Bookstore*

Winner of the Anna Seghers Prize (2018)

Winner of the José Saramago Literary Prize for *Resistance* (2017)

Winner of the Jabuti Award for Book of the Year for *Resistance* (2016)

Winner of the Oceanos Prize for Literature in Portuguese for *Resistance* (2016)

OCCUPATION

First published by Charco Press 2021
Charco Press Ltd., Office 59, 44-46 Morningside Road, Edinburgh
EH10 4BF

Copyright © Julián Fuks 2019
First published in Portuguese as *A Ocupação*
English translation copyright © Daniel Hahn 2021

A CIP catalogue record for this book is available from the British
Library.

ISBN: 9781916277878
e-book: 9781916277885

www.charcopress.com

Copy Editor: Francisco Vilhena
Senior Editor: Fionn Petch
Designer: Pablo Font
Typesetter: Laura Jones
Proofreader: Fiona Mackintosh

2 4 6 8 10 9 7 5 3 1

Supported using public funding by
ARTS COUNCIL
ENGLAND

LOTTERY FUNDED

Julián Fuks

OCCUPATION

Translated by
Daniel Hahn

CHARCO PRESS

For my father

He was waiting for the barbarians as if he were waiting for himself. He wanted to be invaded. He wanted to be conquered, occupied from head to foot, to the point of forgetting who he had been before the invasion.

Mia Couto, *Women of the Ashes*
(trans. by David Brookshaw)

There is no such thing as someone's blood. With every person who loses blood, we all bleed.

Mia Couto, *The Sword and the Spear*
(trans. by David Brookshaw)

1.

Every man is the ruin of a man, I might have thought. This man who appeared before my eyes was an incarnation of that maxim, a creature in precarious condition, a body submerged within its own debris. This impression didn't come from his thin neck, his wretched torso, his twisted legs on the wheelchair, but from a lesser, circumstantial feature: the man at that moment was the ruin of a man because he was completely intoxicated. I could tell by the words he repeated, by the truncated sentences, by the voice which was itself the ruin of a voice. I didn't look at his eyes, I didn't get the chance to look into his eyes to see my own image.

I might have thought it, but I didn't think it because we were walking together, she and I side by side, we were walking towards the centre across that city we believed belonged to us. The man placed that wreck of a wheelchair in our way and asked, unexpectedly polite, if we might push him to the next corner. I didn't even need to check with her this time. I took hold of the two handles behind the man and pointed him in the right direction, struggling with the wheels against the precariousness of the pavement.

When we reached halfway, the man stopped us with a broad wave of his arm. He could get to the corner later, what he wanted now was to have a shot of cachaça at this bar just here. He asked us to buy him that cachaça. At this point it's possible that we, she and I, exchanged glances. The man was too drunk, a cachaça might cloud what little consciousness still remained in him, a cachaça would surely flood the wreckage of him. And yet it was obvious this man must live a life of unimaginable pain, personal or familial pain, physical or spiritual pain, pain that deserved to be diluted in as much alcohol as possible.

The two of us left the man on the pavement and disappeared into the darkness of that ruin of a bar. I already had the cachaça in my left hand, my only ten-real note in my right, when I heard somebody addressing her, somebody else had something they wanted to ask us for. It was a boy who was too young to be the ruin of a boy, too young to be his own ruin. He was thirsty, that's what he said in his high-pitched voice, he was just asking us to buy him some juice or other. The request was fair and precise, but I couldn't help feeling there was something improper in the obvious swap, something immoral about breaking the promise we had made to the man, allowing the boy's need to assert itself over the man's desire.

The dilemma was a small one, I knew that, our city's perverseness manifest in insignificance, a squalor replicated daily all around the world, on an infinite number of street corners. But all the same I found myself paralysed. In the darkness, I couldn't make out her expression, and for a moment I felt, though I said nothing, that the word I spoke would be my ruin.

2.

I wasn't thinking about whether the man was the ruin of a man when I arrived to see my father. I wasn't thinking about anything. I saw his body being transported on a stretcher, I heard the wheels squeaking against the floor of the corridor, I noticed the serious expressions on the faces of the nurses who were pushing him. In the shadows cast against the hospital walls, his silhouette seemed to take on extraordinary dimensions. My father had grown, as if the illness that afflicted him were expanding his outlines, as if the misfortune were increasing the space he occupied in the world. Only later did the doctor explain, squeezing that enormous arm with her hard fingers: the punctured lung allowed the air he inhaled to escape, so it spread beneath his skin, producing a general swelling.

I felt no such swelling in my mother's back. As I hugged her, my palms flat against her shoulder blades, I felt exactly the opposite, as if her bones were lacking in flesh, as if I were hugging nothing. My mother at that moment was a more haggard woman, a body too slender to accept my embrace. Our bodies parted as though nothing were parting, and I wanted to tell her something that in the end I could not. There was a kind of hardness in her features, a kind of harshness in her voice, and I knew her well enough to decipher these scarce signs. In my mother, the impatience that was so uncommon in her concealed an uncertainty, a bad mood served to hide her fragility.

I spent the night alone in the hospital, though alone is not quite the right word. Somebody once defined solitude as a sweet absence of looks, but not that night. That night, the squares of glass in the door of the room were two eyes peering at me, stealing my privacy while at the same time providing me with no company; sometimes a sleeping man can be the deepest absence of all. My solitude that night was a fear of solitude, a fear of seeing that greater space he occupied now, in the world, in the room, in me, transformed into emptiness.

In the small hours, unable to sleep, I moved my armchair closer to his bed. I pressed my finger against his bulky arm and felt an unexpected softness, and noticed the white outline of my finger marked on his red skin. That air wasn't the problem, that air would dissipate in time, said the doctor. A noisy piece of equipment was already busy extracting the excess emptiness from his body, the wind that had invaded him and separated him from his own cells. He looks like a startled frog, somebody said. He looks like a Chinese wise man. I rejected any idea that took him away from what he was, or what I saw in him, any description that made him anything other than my father. The equipment continued to fulfil its function, noisily. All the same, I found myself moving the palm of my hand across his forearm, several times in succession, thinking that in this way I might revive his pores, and the invading wind would fade away that was distancing him from himself.

3.

In the morning the abrasive sun fired up my pores and within a few blocks I was already sweating, already feeling my body dissolve into the unpleasant, dry weather. The excessive light made every unfamiliar face look murky, or perhaps it was my own face that looked murky, reflected in the shop windows like an anonymous shapeless thing, my body no more than a silhouette. With weak fingers I held onto the piece of paper on which I had written the address, 210 Avenida Nove de Julho, but my blurry feet were unable to locate the correct destination. I walked through the first door I could find and into a dazzling entrance hall. Is this the Cambridge Hotel, I asked, already preparing the statement that would follow, I've come to visit a guest. From a still featureless face I heard the answer, whispered with an indiscreet laugh: The Cambridge Hotel no longer exists, the hotel that used to exist closed down a long time ago.

That, as if in some poor mystery adventure novel, was my first contact with the old hotel, or what was no longer left of it. Barely more than twenty paces away the mystery was dispelled, cancelled by the tall building's solidity, by its concrete pillars. I didn't expect anybody to open the heavy door, which had an iron bolt across it, but a lad with a neutral expression let me through without too many questions. I wrote my name on a piece of paper on a clipboard, my details, and with this very simple gesture I felt myself returning to myself: Sebastián, no longer shapeless, no longer an anonymous man wandering austere streets.

It was only then, situated in my body, that I began to understand the space surrounding me, that haven of shadows where my eyes rested from the outside glare. There was no longer a hotel, and yet here its imposing entrance hall held out, its whitewashed walls, stripped of any adornment, its ceiling unreachable over my head. There was no longer a hotel, and yet its stairs rose up step by step, stones polished by the ceaseless friction of the days. There was no longer a hotel, and yet its doors hid an infinite number of bodies that were just as solid as my own, through their doors seeped almost inaudible voices, voices that came to me on the move, voices that kept me in motion.

When I reached the eighth floor, when I found the door shut, I did not lack the strength to close my fist and strike the wood.

4.

They tell me you write about exile, about lives adrift, about trees whose roots are buried thousands of kilometres away, he said in that harsh accent of his, the hoarseness aggravated by the static on the telephone line. Yes, I've written about an exile, that was the only part of what he'd said that I dared to confirm, as I tried to take in the strangeness of that image, the monstrous tree that doesn't lose its roots even when brutally lopped off. I would have hinted at a correction, I think, I would have said that such distances always elude my words, that I've written about things that are close and personal, but I was unable to challenge his assertiveness with my hesitancy. His voice seemed to resound from within that strange tree: I have a story to tell you, meet me at the Cambridge Hotel, eighth floor.

And so, there I found myself, standing in front of that man who let me in with no effusiveness, a livid face welcoming me into his home with little more than a slight sagging of his eyelids. No, walking through that doorway would not mean coming to know his home. Nothing particularly his own was reflected in that realm of such scarcity, nothing personal in the few objects soberly dispersed. Only what looked like a light blanket thrown over the sofa, a red blanket with oriental patterning, broke the austerity with its bright colour, yet even such a bright red paled in the grey mildness of that setting. The blanket was where we sat, and I tried to silence these thoughts, and he began to speak.

His name was Najati, he came from Syria, he had been exiled in São Paulo for a few months, although nobody had authorised the word for him, he didn't expect the solemnity of exile, as he lacked the official designation. Najati was a refugee, one of five million Syrians now abroad. One of the many wandering the world with their hands over their ears, he said, their hands blocking out the noise of the bombs exploding in the distance, which never stop exploding. He came from Homs, he came from a house hidden by orange trees. At the foot of an orange tree he said goodbye to his sons who were going to be piling up rocks in Qatar, and he saw his wife for the last time – his wife who today hears only the bombs, who no longer hears the oranges dropping onto the dry earth. His wife's wave, growing further and further away in the dry fog, in the dust, at the foot of an orange tree, that was what he saw for the last time as the police car turned the corner.

This was my crime, he said, and on the screen of his cellphone I could see him for the first time looking energetic and rejuvenated – the six-minute sequence I would watch so many times on my own, shut away in my study, listening carefully to that incomprehensible language, not understanding why I was doing it, why on some free evenings I do it still. Najati in the middle of a circular plaza, atop an improvised stage, surrounded on all sides by a huge crowd of brightly coloured flags, nodding heads, arms raised to applaud him after each ever more intense line. That was 2012, it was spring, explained the aged Najati when the other one no longer had anything to say. It was a spring afternoon, the beginning of hope and the beginning of the end, on that same afternoon, at the same time, indistinguishable.

Of the story that followed, about the years he spent in a tent crammed full of common criminals and political prisoners, likewise indistinguishable, about his premature release on condition he left the country immediately, with what remained of his clothing and his fibre, of the story that followed, what I have retained is mostly the bitter taste of the tea he offered me. It didn't seem reasonable to ask for sugar in the middle of that narrative, interrupting him as he described the persistent blows that left their marks on his body, the panic of the other men, in the dead of night, as they crossed the vast sea in a tiny boat. I don't know why it seems reasonable for me to interrupt him now, mentioning the tea, mentioning the sugar, and not to ask myself whether the sharp furrows I could see on his face, wrinkles like deep rivers, were not marks from the same ill-treatment, and whether that same panic wasn't still hidden in his eyes beneath those drooping lids.

Sitting there, my gaze flicking between his ruddy face and the red blanket, between his dark face and the darkness of the tea, it was only there that I wondered what this man might be expecting of me. What tiny benefit might he get from confessing to the guy who I was to him, a foreigner and a stranger, about his banishment, his private desert? What impossible word could give him any relief, some sterile comfort? Or was an author for his story what he wanted, and was that his hope, was that his purpose for me in the end? Sitting there, incapable of silencing my thoughts, I don't know if I'd already come to think that ultimately all men are the ruin of a man. I know I saw him through the dry fog of my eyes, I saw him for the first time, and I thought for the first time that this was not a man, it was not a man, merely the ruins of one.

5.

And for us, could that unremarkable spring night have been the beginning of hope or did it confirm the beginning of the end? This time we were walking again towards the centre, I can't imagine we held hands, we didn't exchange glances. Perhaps the wind blew through our hair with some leftover trace of winter, maybe the last. She didn't hold me back with the palm of her hand on my forearm, I don't think anything changed in the pace of our steps, she didn't wait for us to arrive at any particular corner. We need to decide, she said, her voice firm, and so stable, we need to decide if we're having a child, or not.

For more than a decade, the certainty of that not had been one of her most emphatic convictions. Ever since university I had heard her assert, to those who were most insistent and inappropriate, that she didn't want children, she'd never wanted children, she was never going to want children, that a woman didn't need to have a child to experience any kind of completeness, and how stupid it was, this stubborn reduction of the feminine to maternity. I admired that verve, I liked witnessing her interlocutors' unease, the way they felt compelled to contradict such firmness and ended up getting lost in claims they couldn't sustain. I might have kept quiet, it was expected of me that I keep quiet, but the truth is that I was drawn to much more than those words, I was drawn to her conviction, to her ability to maintain a certainty with such fervour. And yet, I wanted children, I'd always wanted children, I was always going to want children, I believed, and I believed contrary to all logic that one day I would convince her to join me in that desire.

In recent years, with the greatest discretion, her certainty had begun to grow less emphatic, then less certain, gradually taking on the outlines of an ever more deferred doubt. One day, who knows, maybe ten years from now, or seven, or five, she'd say in passing at moments of intimacy, while her body showed no indication of tiredness, while her back revealed no sign of the extra weight. On that spring night, then, on that night when the wind blew with the last remaining trace of winter, when she stated that we needed to decide if we were going to have a child or not, at that moment, I could not be in any way surprised, and I understood without a shadow of a doubt that there was no one to convince, there was nothing to decide.

6.

There was something that needed saying on those first days, I knew there was something that needed saying, but the words wouldn't come to my aid. Sitting in the armchair that I had returned to its original position, I spent the long hospital hours on fake distractions, I would look down at the book of the day and scan entire pages without taking in a single idea, without a single image coming to mind. I'm lying. Most of the time I had my face blurry in the light of my cellphone, lost in countless news articles about the latest national convulsion, as dramatic and transient as all the others – comprising and concealing the bigger picture, the country's gradual return to its authoritarian past. In the profusion of someone else's words, perhaps I was playing down the paucity of my own. Maybe I was reading so as not to look at my father's face.

His voice, however, did not escape me. It was a much higher-pitched voice than usual, the sound of air forcing itself out against the air itself, swelling his vocal cords. It was as if he had inhaled an enormous helium balloon and could only talk in that funny way, someone said, but any amusement was beyond my reach. It was as if he himself was the balloon and might take off at any moment, leaving the bed empty and floating towards the ceiling, but not even in fantasy did I want to witness this solid man lift. In those first days, his inert body in that bed was the only thing I could cling to, the solid body in the bed was what I could still call my father.

His voice, however, did not escape me. Not because of its unusually high pitch, but the irritation that could be heard in everything he said, in the limited series of words that he stitched laboriously together. His back hurt, he complained. His chest hurt. The hospital room was cold. The noise of the machine that was constantly sucking on his skin was intolerable. When I was freed at last from distractions, I saw in his swollen face all the discomfort that had been manifest in his voice, saw his eyebrows furrowed in the most private displeasure, eyebrows that were untamed and tousled, I saw his waning eyes, already worn out from so much unease. None of this was normal for him; in this muddle of disquiets I struggled to recognise the familiar figure of my father.

That wasn't my father, I remember accepting it for a moment. Our whole lives we look at a father's face and see the most varied emotions, the most different affections, love, distress, tiredness, nervousness, but not every face becomes characteristic, and not every expression becomes his synthesis. My father was, to me, at least up until then, the figure of a man engrossed, lost in private journeys. My father was calm above all, he had the serenity of those who are truly distracted. My father was a guy who twenty years earlier had been freed of himself, the man with a cigarette in hand, drawing in a profound pleasure from that cigarette, drawing in the world with his timid eyes. That man existed only in photographs, it was he who was guilty of the fate of this other man now pinned to the bed, and perhaps I ought to feel resentful.

All the same, as I felt overtaken by my father's disquiet, I remember that I could not deny the desire I felt to offer him a cigarette, to see him once again engrossed, drawing in the serenity of the world once again. No, I contradicted myself, my desire was not to give him a cigarette, that could not possibly have been my desire. What I wanted was the opportunity to snatch a cigarette from his lips, as if I were thereby snatching death from out of his mouth.

7.

My father was a militant, he lived a secret life. I have already told the story of his militancy, his struggle in a distant decade against the authoritarianism established in his country, I've already described the persecution he endured, his existence shaken by politics. I have already squandered words about resistance when recounting the final secret meeting in which he took part – before he had children, before he left for exile in Brazil, before he stopped smoking, before he became a peaceable being and unlearnt the daring of his youthful acts. Before he made utopia into a mere intellectual speculation, I go on, before he allowed himself to cultivate worldly comforts, before his body began its decline, before this son saw him prostrate in a private hospital bed and, out of sadness, helplessness, rage, could accuse him wordlessly of capitulating, of surrendering to the pettinesses of life – as if unaware that he had no one to accuse but himself.

But I was thinking about none of this, none of this baffled me while I was a part of that gathering of atypical militants, with the sense that I too was a militant, that I too was living a secret life. I did not yet fully understand why I accepted the second invitation from Najati, why I was once again being drawn into the dilapidation of the centre, why I was trying to camouflage my too-white skin in a blush, why, from what, I was taking refuge in that non-existent hotel. The voices I had heard days earlier behind the doors now took on visible faces, tangible outlines, bruising gestures. The hubbub they created, I felt momentarily, seemed to surround my silence and embrace it.

Preta, from number 42, huge hair accentuating the smallness of her face, eyes in that small face that were animated and happy, in a dissonance with what she had to say: the water comes out murky in the lower floors, the water is dirty with mud perhaps, dirty with old dust, we're going to have to clean out the plumbing. Sandra, from 33, hands and chin resting on the broom with which she has just cleaned the vast expanse of cement: the fencing around the elevator shaft needs reinforcing, if a kid trips on that, I don't know if it mightn't just collapse completely once and for all. Antônio, from 105, feet firmly planted on the floor, solid legs apart: the business with Brito needs checking; ever since the forklift dumped a whole ton on his leg, it's been taking him more than half an hour just on the staircase to the tenth floor.

When I had begun to enjoy that litany of emergencies, when the building's murky water was already starting to cleanse my transparencies, when my abstractions were already giving way beneath the whole huge weight of that present life, a shriller voice cut across the hall of that old hotel. Guys, this is not the place for dealing with matters like those. That's why we have our regular meetings, our assemblies. If I called you all together on an unscheduled night it's because the situation's serious, you can't just go talking about trivial stuff like this. In this situation here, we're talking about a step backwards, about repression, about a loss of rights. You can't just stay shut up in here arguing, quibbling over the finer points, over aesthetic details.

It was Carmen who was speaking, a stocky body, a serious demeanour. That massive figure had an authority to her I had rarely witnessed before, an authority I had never heard from my father, an authority I myself would never attain with my attachment to hesitation and uncertainty. And then, making us all equal in our silence, Carmen began to recount an ancient night, recalled by so many here, when everything they had was devastated, when a construction of years collapsed to the ground in a matter of hours, under the weight of uniforms and nightsticks. Or rather, the building remained standing, static, empty, indifferent, and what collapsed to the ground were the two hundred families who lived there, fleeing out onto the avenue with their mattresses on their heads, spending the early hours of that morning, and the next mornings, and the next, under a flyover crowded with people.

How many here had experienced that night? How many here remember? Those who did not experience it ought to listen to their companion's words, because history can repeat itself in very short order. There's already an arrest warrant against me, she went on, folded up in the pocket of a starched uniform for them to use whenever they feel like it. There's already a repossession order for the Cambridge, stored away in the drawer of some suit-wearer or other. But we no longer answer warrants now, we don't respond to orders, we won't allow ourselves to be brought down without a struggle, not without any resistance.

That was what I had to say, that was why I wanted everyone here together, militants and refugees – whether refugees in their own countries or a foreign one, because that's what we are, it doesn't matter which land you're in. They want to have us be tramps, they want to have us be bandits, ragamuffins, paupers, they want us to lack everything, country, land, a house to live in, a bit of ground to die on. That's their mistake: they don't know we are all of us refugees, they don't know how much strength refugees have for maintaining their grip on the rock, how deep the roots of exile go. So they can all start getting ready, because a flower is going to grow out of the concrete, and that flower is red.

Glued to my chair, unmoving while everything became movement, I was trying to understand how a piece of information like this could be received so energetically, how this expected defeat could be transformed into immediate action. Unmoving, glued to my chair, I only noticed Najati's approach when he was already beside me, a tangible body, neither whole nor decrepit, and I was as startled as if I'd been beside my own father, now or in some other time. Without saying a word, paying no attention to my surprise, Najati merely handed me an envelope.

8.

For more than a decade there were two of us in the same house, only two. Between us two, from night to night, it seemed impossible that we should not create an ultimate closeness, an intimacy greater than each of us experiences when alone, when abandoned. Between us two, there was too much house, all we were interested in was the room being occupied, as if all other rooms did not exist or were locked. Between us two, from night to night, for over a decade, it seemed impossible that we should not compose a shared encyclopaedia of ideas, an anthology of actions, an atlas of gestures, a dictionary of private words. Using this never-published bibliography we would continue to apply our mutual pedagogy, teaching each other to be alike, to be just one, a single adjacent body with ordinary habits – even if it was written in the non-existent encyclopaedia, in an entry that she drafted, that we needed to be two, that we needed to be whole, never two inadequate halves, never those pathetic lovers that dissolve their singularity in the delusion of love.

And then we wanted to be three, and in order to be three we needed to be two once again. Merely wanting to be three was enough for us to feel the visit of a third, an intruder between us, a stranger, a secret. It was in secret that we would make a child, nobody would have to know right away, and the secrecy served simultaneously to distinguish us from others and restore us to ourselves – we were two accomplices in an unexpected act, in an extravagant act, in the most common human act of all. That elation was not a thing we shared, each of us experienced an elation of our own, and each saw the other's elation and felt requited – we were two people executing the most ambitious, most beautiful of plans. Nor did we share our uncertainty, our concern, our fear, and this was something we did not want to see in the other's face, these words were banned for a time from our dictionary.

And then there was the sex, I don't know why I almost never write about the sex. From night to night, for more than a decade, it seemed impossible that sex should not become habitual, a compendium of automated actions, undoubtedly pleasurable, irreparably efficient. A word or a gesture were enough for the other to understand, an afternoon nap, or fingers lightly brushing along a leg, sometimes the simple switching between rooms at a suspect time of day, to start up the sequence of familiar, objective, correct touches and movements – like a body that has touched itself for so many years that it now claims total control over itself, and no longer contemplates the discovery of new points of sensitivity. And then, with the intruder between us, this amalgamated body split for a moment. Perhaps at that time it was already the disparity, already the distance, but as it turned out for a few months we were able to go back to experiencing the delights of difference, the pleasure of friction, the bliss of strangeness.

9.

My whole life I've hardly ever witnessed the final muteness, the silence of death. All of the instances of death that surrounded my so very un-tragic existence, it occurs to me now, were related to my father. Of my paternal grandparents I knew little or nothing. When I was born, their deaths were distant facts that had already stopped leaving any grief – or no more than a discreet resentment on the part of my father, at having lost his mother's warmth in the cold years of childhood. Of the previous generations what reverberated was upper-case death, superlative death, massive and arbitrary death, but that was something we never spoke of.

The first death that reached me in the present was that of my aunt, my father's only sister. It happened, at least for me, on a Saturday morning. My mother came into the bedroom, sat down beside me on the bed, put her hand on my shoulder and announced that she had some bad news. Aida isn't doing well, we're going to Argentina. You'll stay with your brother and sister, and we'll be back in three days. I answered that it was fine, we'd manage, and stayed lying there, regretting the disruption to the weekend, and remembering too the good Sundays I had enjoyed with Aida, years before, on walks that introduced me to a more playful Buenos Aires than the grey, sullen city of my parents. Maybe she was the closest thing I had to a grandmother: her soft voice, her slow walk, her eyes like a sea into which all calm seemed to flow. I don't know how long it took me to find it strange: if Aida was merely unwell, and if it was serious enough for them to leave in a hurry, how could they already know for sure when they would be coming back? From the hallway I caught sight of my father, framed by the door to his bedroom, shoulders more hunched than usual, face fallen, eyes turned towards some corner I knew was empty, staring into the density of nothing. At that moment I was sure about her death and I froze, not knowing how to approach him and give him a hug, and receive one from him, and say the word that would be up to the expected response I was lacking.

Now I was looking at my father in the hospital bed and my mother's words echoed: he isn't doing well. I had my father just a few steps away from me, and, since that first night when I happened casually to caress his arm, I had been almost unable to touch him. I returned, after so many years, to that Saturday morning: my father distressed before my eyes, facing the cruelty of time, the vertigo of sudden non-existence. No common-place could satisfy us at that moment. Death was not yet established, maybe death was not even going to establish itself, but I was already unable to prevent its silence from exerting its power over me.

10.

And then there was the day we said goodbye to Tango. That might perhaps have been a less sudden and brief death, having been slowly anticipated by small afflictions, gradual revelations of another's suffering, a subtle learning of the inescapable nothingness when one is confronted with pain.

When Tango arrived home, he was life itself incarnate, a non-stop frenzy of movement, weaving paths between our legs, tiny teeth ripping our socks, the hems of our trousers. For a few days, he transformed the family into a single collective laughter. When he was no longer a puppy, and when the scratches on our legs started to be a nuisance, Tango was moved into the garden and our laughing became shyer. Only my father was in the habit of spending time regularly outside with him. Through the window I could see him for long periods stroking the black and gold fur, sharing confidences with the dog that I would never hear.

I didn't often want to go with them on walks around the neighbourhood. It was vivid in my memory, and it still is, that first time I saw him sprawled on the sidewalk against the railings of another house, his dog body pure trembling, eyes almost closed with agony and stress, a thick white foam coming from his mouth. I don't know how long the fit lasted, I know I watched it through eyes as narrowed as the animal's. Tango is epileptic, my father said gently, as if the mere word might bring some measure of relief, but it did not. My father then put his arm around me, made us crouch down, and started to stroke the animal's panting body, the pale belly inflating and deflating. To the slow cadence of the gesture he explained each symptom, either to me or to the dog, in the serenest voice he could manage. It didn't take long for us, for Tango and me, to calm down. It was only when it was all over that I noticed, curious, that the epileptic fit had taken place opposite the garden where Tango's parents had lived, a thin set of railings away from the exact point where he had come into the world. But I never knew what to make of this; perhaps it was no more than a coincidence, since my father on his walks was always passing by that house.

On another morning I was awoken by the insistence of my father's shouts, shouts that were deep and getting louder, dramatic in his Spanish pronunciation: Tango, Tango, Tango. Through the window I saw him rummaging about in the most unlikely corners of the garden, though already hopeless of finding him hidden there. Then we set off in opposite directions, both of us looking for the dog, and now I was the one shouting in my unstable adolescent voice: Tango, Tango, Tango. When I came back, my father was trying to hold him in a hug, trying not to touch his bloodied tail, crushed by an automatic garage door a few blocks from our house, the house he had wanted to run away from. He whined as though he had gone back to being a puppy, like those first nights when we had shut him on the other side of the door. He was suffering. He was suffering so badly that he couldn't help himself and he sank his teeth into my father's arm, with all his fury, sharing his suffering with him, arm and dog fused in the same pain. A pain I couldn't even imagine, as I still cannot, as nobody is able to imagine any pain. With lifeless feet and clenched fists, all I could manage was distress.

In his final months, Tango was an apathetic creature who no longer scratched legs, or leapt fences, and barely wagged the stump of tail he had left. The remains of so many former sufferings seemed to be concentrated in one specific point on his back, the point from which his body lost its elegant bearing, the point where his spine bent at an angle he must have found terribly uncomfortable. Since he did not whine and he did not bark, since he did not even have the spirit to reveal his suffering, I could spend days without it occurring to me to look out the window, protecting myself from his deterioration, wanting, perhaps, to evade pity and sympathy.

Then one day my father asked me to go with him. Tango wasn't doing well, something needed to be done. It's a sad situation, the only option for him is euthanasia, he explained on the way to the veterinary clinic, and at that moment the word seemed devoid of any morbidity, no worse than an unpleasant medicine, a curative act like any other. The three of us shut ourselves in a sterile room, though I remained slightly apart, watching my father's arm as he stroked the dog, the mark of canine teeth on that arm, two round scars as red as blood. I don't remember the words my father said at that farewell, I don't remember the ones I said next. I remember feeling that a solitude was beginning there, albeit a partial and nostalgic one, just one more solitude among the others my father had accumulated over the course of his life. I remember feeling that, on the way back home, my company wouldn't be worth much to him.

11.

From out of the envelope Najati gave me I drew the sheets of white paper, one by one, which had been placed inside with obvious care. All in all, there were no more than thirty pages. They were stories, or columns, or autobiographical accounts, possibly a single fragmentary narrative, constituting an imperfect, unfinished whole. The text was aligned right, as in the original Arabic, and translated into a precarious English, in which article and noun might merge into a single impossible word, and very often the author had deduced the spelling of certain words from their sound. It was a piece of writing with an accent, the same accent I had heard in his deep voice, in that voice that was potent but hoarse, as though a new language were being born from out of its hoarseness. As I read the text, I felt something resembling what I felt when we talked, that his accent, so saturated with the past, was denouncing the unseemly precision I sought with mine, my apathetic surrender to the foreign pronunciation made of uncomfortable vowels and tongue between teeth.

What thrummed from the pages, however, once the linguistic obstacles had been overcome, after the noise of the words had been silenced, was their extreme candour and simplicity. In Najati's texts Syria was not there to be read, at first the war was not there to be read, or the destruction, the greatest ruin in its historic scale. It was in the everyday trivialities that the vastness of the misery was revealed. In the possessing of the body and in its dispossession, in the deprivation of the body or of everything else, and in the unforeseen value attained by each trivial little object that he still possessed.

Abou Sabouna, that was the title given to the first piece of writing, referring to the nickname earned by one of his fellow inmates. No soap was made available in that prison, nor anything but dirty water for washing in, but Najati managed to bring a bar of soap in among his essential medicines. Every night he forced himself not to go to sleep, he remained awake as long as he could, and then slipped away to the bathroom without anyone seeing him. In the small hours of the morning he would furiously wash his whole body, he would scrub his legs, chest, shoulders and arms hard – washing himself was perhaps the most certain way of recovering his dignity, of finding himself again. One night, however, one of the other prisoners heard and followed him to the bathroom. The other prisoner easily discovered his secret, he didn't need to insist for Najati to lend him the soap – if he hadn't wanted to be seen in such a commonplace act, it was because he sensed how readily he would accede to this request. Abou, however, was a clumsy lad, that's what the narrator says. So desperate was he to wash that with his first movement the soap slipped from his hands and disappeared down the drain. The two men jumped, other men came over, the moment became the source of much laughter, and in that dirty water with no soap – no *saboun* – the lad received his new name.

The second text was harder to define. It began like an extract from an instruction manual detailing how and where to buy a refrigerator in Homs, with the consumer-to-be given two options. If he wanted a new product with a guarantee, he should seek out, on those shopping streets that were still in operation, those stores that had not yet been blown up. But if he didn't have the money this required, he should go to the so-called Sunni market, a Homs innovation that had spread across the country. There the consumer would find all manner of used products, household appliances, utensils, ornaments, photo albums which very conveniently already had photos of couples and children included.

The story's narrator or the writer of the article then assumes a gloomier tone and drops the advertising language. These are the belongings of many Sunni families who've been plundered by the regime, especially those families whose members had protested in favour of freedom, they are the objects that populated all those destroyed houses, the destroyed memories, the lives. The Sunni refrigerator is the symbolic synthesis of the Syrian question, here the narrator turns grandiloquent, it's the most concrete expression of the systemic eradication of the Sunni people. The lighter tone resurfaces at the end: if somebody at one of those markets should happen to buy an old fridge, light yellow, large, with two doors, a Brazilian make, which has already had its motor replaced several times, let him at least spare a thought for the author of this text and he will be immediately forgiven.

I was reading these texts and I was not thinking about the author; I was thinking about literature itself, or thinking about myself. How forcefully those pages struck me, perhaps incomprehensibly, when they immersed me in their atmosphere of pain and devastation. It had been a while since literature had had that effect on me, it never transcended its wearisome games, its conceits, its childish enticements. It had been a while since literature had shown itself so urgent and expressive. The impression wouldn't last any time at all, I knew that, the moment would immediately stretch out to dissipate its intensity. Here, all the same, I did believe I had found an unlikely ideal of writing, and wished that someday Najati's pages might come to occupy my own.

12.

The most natural of human acts, I might have insisted. No, even more than that, the most natural act of all, human or otherwise, so close to the very definition of naturalness. We are young, we are healthy, we've only been trying a few months, no reason we should be worried. There's no reason we should mistrust our own bodies, no reason to hurry what ought to be simple, organic, almost banal. I was the one talking at that moment, she was just listening to me, neither of us could understand my agitation, my excitement. Why, I was saying, why would we attack our bodies with embarrassing tests, with exogenous hormones, with unnecessary medication. What's with this desire to manage what is averse to all management, what's with this inclination to medicalise life?

We're not as young as all that, Sebastián, she might have said. Open your eyes to what's happening around us, forget about that vanity of yours, that omnipotence, for a while. Everywhere there are couples struggling to get pregnant, wasting years on fruitless efforts. It seems to get harder and harder, slower, more and more uncertain, even if pregnancies on the first attempt do happen now and then, and accidental pregnancies, those unusual figures that denounce the sterility of our own advances. There's nothing banal about the frustration that descends every month, staining that day and all the days that follow. Please understand, what I'm proposing isn't some kind of attack, it isn't implying any mistrust. I just thought we might check that everything's in order, and, you never know, perhaps take a little something that might help us make it.

Every month, in the days leading up to the negative, our life would be transformed into a constant oscillation of moods, a torrent of speculations and uncertainties. She felt a strange weight in her lower belly, a pressure making its presence felt there: she must be pregnant. No, it would only take a few hours for her to correct herself, the weight had something fluid about it, it's a liquid weight, a forewarning of blood discharge: she wasn't pregnant. She would feel a strange hunger, as if something beyond her were revealing its cravings, as if her body or another body might be making demands on her at any hour to be fed: she must be pregnant. No, wait, the hunger is almost a diffuse pain in her stomach and spreading around her back, almost a colic, or a prediction of the colic that was on its way: she wasn't pregnant. She felt a strange sleepiness, more frequent and more intense than usual, as if it was essential that she rest: she must be pregnant. No, on that same night, insomnia occupied her early hours and sleep became a suffocating impossibility, a lesser expression of another impossibility: she wasn't pregnant.

Early in the morning, her hand shook my shoulder with a mixture of tenderness and tension. Today I didn't dream I was pregnant. I dreamt I was a mother, to a baby who was as yet faceless, sexless, nameless. We had a hammock on the living room wall and we were rocking, the boy and me, the girl and me, gently swinging against a backdrop of motionless trees, motionless buildings, a motionless sky. I listened to her with a mixture of tension and tenderness, never wondering why I had no place in that scene, in that hammock, why it wasn't me breaking the motionlessness of that landscape. What I did wonder, with very slight anxiety, without finding the words, was why I never dreamt I was a father.

13.

I knocked on Najati's door, he didn't answer. I turned around and contemplated the many doors offered in series, some of them ajar, feeling the impulse to knock on some door or other, to hear some story or other, but not daring to do it. I walked down the stairs slowly, I didn't want to leave so early, and stepped back into the hallway of another floor to allow some children, announced by their piercing clamour, to get past me. They leaped from step to step with agile, joyful legs, they had no idea what the future held for them, I thought and reprimanded myself for thinking it. The last of them, the girl who was the smallest in the group, stopped and asked my name. She was surprised at my reply for a moment, but then she made a gesture of scorn as if I was kidding, she said welcome and continued down the stairs with her friends.

Nobody has ever said welcome to me in my building, that was what I thought when she disappeared from view. In my building, like in so many others, cordiality demands no more than a nod of the head along the corridors, or small talk in the elevators, brief sentences that can even do without names. For years these encounters get repeated, reconciled to their irrelevance, and the faces get older without becoming any more intimate. There in the occupation, I thought I understood, the daily passing on the stairs seemed to encourage encounters that were slowed down, and thus more alive, as if in sharing the same breath those people saw themselves as sheltered from haste, from a lack of interest, from indifference. That wasn't something that occurred to me right away: without understanding why I was doing it, I found myself coming down and up the stairs countless times, and laughing at my own tiredness whenever somebody mirrored my laughter.

On the upper floors, encounters became rarer and the space seemed gloomier. On the fifteenth floor, the last one, a doorless opening led out onto a terrace without railings, unadorned dark concrete against the grey sky. I thought I would allow my eyes to lose themselves in the infinite, or in the unequal finitude of the indistinct buildings, but my attention came to rest upon the other side of the avenue, on an already very familiar façade. It was the Joelma Building, the setting of the great São Paulo tragedy, the fire that had consumed its walls, transforming it into a skeleton, from whose jutting bones so many inhabitants had leapt into the void. For a moment this image was recreated in my mind, as if the building were yet burning, even in the stillness, even in the silence, even with the passing of the decades. What burned once continues to burn, indefinitely – those words passed like a breath over my lips, and I preferred to let them be lost.

I went back inside, but I didn't feel sufficiently protected beneath that roof and I needed to go through another opening, closing the door behind me, already taking off my shoes as if I were entering my own apartment. It was a modest room, visibly abandoned, a chair with torn upholstery next to a Formica counter and a worn old sofa-bed pushed up against the back wall. The sofa was where I went to lie down, raising the dust that reacted to my weight, the grey cloud that enveloped me, or even feeling sheltered in the dusty dome. There, with my eyes closed, I saw myself isolated from the past and the present, removed even from my changeability, from the oscillations of my own mood. A refugee from everything, from the blaze of the world, a refugee from myself.

14.

The gardens that went back to being a cemetery – that was the title. It started with a description of the view he had from the windows of his house, beyond the orange trees, an abundance of eucalyptus and a few rare acacias, he said, that were left after a tree massacre in Ghouta. He continued on a descriptive flight over the gardens, the most beautiful gardens in Homs, passing the mosque on the corner with its sumptuous hall, the modern cultural centre and the Al Mayden road that stretched out the green of the trees as far as the Aboul Laban sweetshop.

In a time that was not long gone, in the place of the gardens there had been a cemetery. The narrator, apparently Najati himself, got personally involved with the transportation of his grandparents' remains to a new graveyard on the outskirts of town, to provide a concrete demonstration that the care of the dead did not require too much solemnity. The park project was facing opposition by those who were most old-fashioned: huge protests advocating for the continued existence of the old cemetery, and everywhere rumours spread about the souls revolting in defence of that space, spirits that broke bulldozers and poisoned workmen. Najati's argument was a simple one, which went against the general obscurantism while still holding on to religious references. The living have priority over the dead. Islam maintains the eternity of souls, not of bodies, which are fated to wither away in spite of their ambitions and their delusions of permanence.

With the street argument won, for years he would visit the gardens even on cold winter evenings, and he would take shelter in the shade of the eucalyptus trees during the electrical blackouts that cut off the fans at the height of the August heat. Though I read no introductions, I felt I knew Najati's family a little: a daughter he had not yet mentioned, Sumayya, and his two grandchildren, Maria and Noos. He and the children used to spend hours in that garden chasing after the birds, all three of them delighted at the serene exuberance of the peacocks. One detail appealed to the reader's sensitivity: his grandchildren's hands tugging on his trousers every morning, their voices calling him enthusiastically, grandpa, grandpa, let's go peacocking – here some greater care might be appropriate in the translation, perhaps.

The shift in the text from playfulness to disaster was a gradual one. Still in that same light tone of the family scene, Najati described how they liked to surprise, in that same garden, the secret agents who were supposed to be following him from afar, breaching the regulation distance and sitting with them on the lower branches beneath the trees. They ended up engaging in lengthy discussions, which never failed to reveal something of the humanity of those agents, good young men when stripped of their uniforms, hardened by the cruel practices their duty demanded of them.

These gardens, as the narrator said he'd lately discovered in an unexpected leap into the present, these gardens had become a military base dotted with obstacles, walls and cement rooms, filled with all kinds of weapons and munitions and tanks and other military gear. The houses of the neighbourhood, his own house among them, were emptied of their inhabitants and plundered, only to be occupied subsequently by army officers or members of the militias. As the years went by, between one clash and another, the whole vicinity was bombed: there is no longer any mosque nor cultural centre, the Al Mayden road leads only to more debris, there's nothing emanating from the sweetshop now but the scent of gunpowder. In a word, announced the narrator despite the fact he was availing himself of more than one, the gardens returned to their original state, becoming a cemetery once again. Or, more serious still, they became a production centre for tombs, for populating cemeteries around the city.

So this text concluded, in the composition of that crude picture of destruction, without the tense humour that had relieved the endings of the previous ones. Here, I felt, the narrator was breaking off because he could no longer speak, he couldn't see any point in speaking, in dwelling on nostalgic trivialities. It was Najati I was looking for in the pages — which I read still hidden away in that bedroom on the top floor of that occupied building, my dusty dome already unmade. I wanted to know more about Najati and his relatives, how much he missed the wife he'd left behind, the children in Qatar, where Sumayya, Maria and Noos were now. I understood, instead, that what he missed the most, his greatest pain, if such pains can be measured, was the pain of knowing that his city had withered away, no longer possessing body nor soul, in spite of its ambitions and its delusions of permanence.

15.

I don't know what to do after death, my father said, and what amazed me was not so much the absurdity of those words but how casually he said them. It had been days since our conversations had gone beyond regular complaints, his high-pitched laments about the body betraying him, my grave laments, which were no doubt insensitive, about the course of a country I no longer recognised. And then, there it was, that unprecedented sentence, which he repeated in a firm voice, in a timbre that was so close to his usual tone: I don't know what to do after death.

The silence was filled up by his ramblings, he didn't know what we should do with his body, what destination to give to what remained of him. No relatives buried in Brazil, in Argentina the few were spread around various cemeteries, no single place in the world that brought his forefathers together, no land that gathered their bones. A sad destiny to be a part of that diaspora. And even if he did return to Argentina, if he was reunited with his sister, then who, after all, would ever visit them? If he'd barely ever made it down south to see her himself, just as he had not visited his mother since growing up, or his father.

If he cannot even grasp a precise meaning for the act of visiting, of resting his eyes on the hard, vacant, impassive stone, of throwing onto the earth a few words that no one will hear. Is that a visit? Him, a psychoanalyst, spending his whole life searching for meanings in the speech of others, contemplating the fairest answer, the most fertile word for cultivating new relationships, new connections, new paths, how could he simply do without listening like this? The one time he was with his sister, in that place where they'd buried her remains, he remembered having been seized by a profound muteness, his lips squeezed together, as if he was never going to be able to speak again.

I listened to him, my mouth pressed shut, unable to add the simplest, the most obvious words, no, dad, it'll all be fine, you don't need to think about things like that, none of that was for me to say, any convention seemed inadequate. Talking was, however, imperative. Saying something. Saying something that evaded the denial and the banality, something that acknowledged his disquiet and his distress. From that suddenly uncomfortable armchair, then, I found myself putting forward possibilities as if the matter demanded a practical solution: perhaps in the garden of his house, in the shade of some familiar tree? And while he retorted that it would be too morbid, especially if we ever wanted to sell the house, a buyer would hardly want a corpse thrown in as a freebie, I just asked myself why that strange suggestion had even occurred to me – without being able to think of Najati, thinking only of Tango, of the visits my father would pay to the dog, of the confidences in the garden that I watched from afar. That might perhaps have been the place where he found the greatest calm, peace radiating from a real intimacy with the place, that was what I was contemplating, and right away I asked myself whether I wasn't the one who wanted a denser piece of earth there in which to confide.

I always imagined you would want to be cremated, I said, changing the course of the conversation. My father always had a digressive sort of rhetorical style, based around twisting sentences that then demanded expansive explanations, seeking complexity, the greatest nuance of meanings, in each idea – synthesis was never one of his virtues. And so, it was with surprise that I received such categorical words, in the voice that had gone back to being high-pitched, the icy pronouncement that echoed in the hospital room and condemned us back into silence: I would never choose to be cremated, I would never finish the job the Nazis started.

16.

In those months, the house was populated with plants. No, the omission of a subject is imprecise: she populated the house with plants, hiding the white walls with a profusion of varying greens, pale and dappled and dark. Each week the house gained new outlines, reflections of light and mosaics of shadow, and the movement of such invasive life was a continuous source of impressions that I could not name. I never could have identified the origin of the change, there was strangeness living in each room and I hadn't realised.

The house wasn't the thing I didn't recognise, that wasn't the source of my uneasiness; the figure who became elusive was her.

The first time we slept together, I remember waking in the middle of the night and leaning over her body, I remember peering through her half-open lips, for no understandable reason, into the darkness inside her mouth. The days diligently assuaged this curiosity I had believed invincible. In the years that followed, we almost always awoke side by side, almost at the same moment, and one would only leave the bedroom when the other showed themselves ready to be awake. The whole relationship seemed to be a pact with constancy, as if the two of us wore the same invisible watch, whose only purpose was to define the time of our presence.

Not now, now my sleep was heavier, opaque, I woke after her. As a vestige of her presence, I found no more than a creased pillow, cold, with a few strands of remaining hair. I would be confronted with her camouflaged shape between the plants, still in pyjamas, a watering can in each hand, in a different place each time, on her silent irrigation circuit. More than once I spotted her crouched down, her face right up close to the earth, eyes shut as if praying, but I assume she was merely listening to a flow that was inaudible to me, the noise of the water making its way through the roots. I never knew what to say to that.

She said one morning, laughing to herself, interrupting my silence: If I can't get pregnant, if at some point I turn into one of those lonely old ladies you find in books, almost invariably the main character's neighbour, I'm not going to be the old cat lady. I want to be the old plant lady. This time I was not lacking in a kind phrase: Don't worry, I'll be around, braving the thick undergrowth in search of you. She was slightly taken aback by the reply, this rather atypical vow did not manage to convince her. I understood through my own words that I no longer claimed to understand her, that she had broken our pact with permanence, with immutability, and that this bothered me to some degree, even as it reawakened my interest.

The following month, the statement was a more surprising one: We need to decide if we're adopting a dog or not. The words had a slightly jocular tone to them, the corners of her mouth trembling with the restraint of a smile. Her fear of dogs was notorious in the family, an unwillingness to live with any kind of pet, so she must be saying something else. Could this be the restating, in a tortuous and redundant way, of her desire to have a child? Now I was the one incapable of an exhaustive sounding-out of the meanings. Now I wasn't thinking about what there was of the elusive in her. I was thinking about myself, and I was thinking about Tango, about his incessant crying up against the window of the old house. I was remembering Tango and the abandonment to which I had subjected him. I was fearing, albeit for one meagre moment, that I would come to abandon my new non-existent dog, too, or my new non-existent child.

17.

First it was the rats. What I mean is, my rat of a husband went first, fifteen years crawling around in the kitchen in search of food, and then some morning he vanished, he gathered whatever clothes he had and went off with another woman. I just lay there, almost dead, sprawled on my bed for hours, unable to feel a thing, pain and sadness and relief were all more than I had the strength for. And so I started to hear the rats, an infestation of rats, running from side to side across the ceiling lining of my house. It wasn't masonry lining, it was plastic, those PVC ones that are really cheap. Do you have any idea how much noise that makes? I bet you've never heard anything like it in your life. The rats ran non-stop over the plastic, they fought one another, made these little shrieking sounds, it echoed everywhere, it was like they were running and fighting and shrieking right inside my ear.

If I did get out of bed it was only because it was unbearable, I needed to call out some exterminators. In those days I was living at the foot of the hill, in Aragominas, and the man had to come out from Araguaína to deal with it. He spent a good while up there laying down the poison, and I was careful to lock Darma, my cat, in the bedroom so she wouldn't get poisoned herself. The man explained how it worked. Rats have a great sense of community, they're like humans: when they find some strange food, they make the weakest or the poorest taste it. An example of unity and solidarity. If that ugly, scrawny little rat survives, all the others can eat in peace. So the poison was not instant. It would only take effect three days later, so that the strong ones, the powerful ones, would die, too.

When the man left, I opened the door to let Darma out and something seemed wrong. There was an unexpected glitter to the bedroom, or no, that wasn't what it was, it was some little blue pellets scattered around the floor, the evil seeds that had spilled through the chinks in the lining. I looked desperately for some trace of that blue on the cat's snout. My certainty that she had eaten the poison, and my terror, were absolute. In those days I'd been reading a lot about Buddhism, I knew that killing any animals was wrong, and yet there I was slaughtering rats. Darma's death would be my punishment, but I didn't accept it. Three days and three nights I spent lying with her on the bed, never taking my hand away from her stomach, I wanted to be with her when the worst happened. On the last night, she trembled all over and seemed to have a spasm, but it was nothing, just a shock from the far side of a dream. Then she woke up, tired of resting, and headed off calmly towards the door.

Then the dead rats started to appear, everywhere. I counted at least twelve in the garden, fallen behind the wardrobe, slipped down the gutter, those unfortunate creatures who'd been unable to flee the massacre. The man didn't want to come back from Araguaína to collect the bodies, so I started burying them one by one in the garden, so that the cat didn't poison herself now and so that they might have some dignity at their end. If I tell you I cried more than once, you and that cold look in your eyes will think I'm exaggerating. But I was crying for everything at once, the son of a bitch who'd gone away, the fear of losing Darma, the wretched end of each of those beings that had once bothered me. I don't know, I think it was my own funeral, too.

I went to sleep and felt like I was sleeping for the first time in days. Yet I woke in the middle of the night with something splattering onto my face, I ran my hand over it and was surprised by the sticky texture. When I turned on the light, I found a whole load of maggots on my bed, on my arms, on my neck, what I had on my face could only be maggots. They were falling from the lamp fitting, a new infestation that was attacking the dead rat infestation. I left the room afraid and found more maggots in the living room, in a long trail across the wall, on the chest of drawers, on the books. You aren't going to believe this, but on one of those Buddhism books they'd gotten inside and seemed to be gnawing on each page. They're revolting, maggots. They smell like whatever they eat, pure carrion spreading around the house. I was sheer rage now, I no longer had a conscience or any pity. I boiled a large pan and started to drown all of the creatures, but the water seemed to make them multiply, it was all living maggots and dead maggots overflowing everywhere. I no longer knew what to do, all I knew was I needed to leave.

You ask why I've ended up here, I couldn't tell you, all I can tell you is why I left there. Arriving at the bus station, I had no place to go, I went into the metro and followed the crowd because I had nobody to follow. My life was a void, made up only of what no longer existed. It was Carmen who got me off the street on those first tough nights in São Paulo, it was the movement that got that dead woman out of me. The fact is, I just got tired of being occupied, by men, by rats, by maggots. Now it's my turn to occupy, don't you think? Rosa, my name's Rosa.

18.

Ever since that last conversation, followed by new days of hospital silence, I no longer stopped looking at my father. The effect of my discomfort was perhaps reversed now: I could no longer turn away, I was neglecting my country's agonies in my inability to abandon his. Everything about his appearance overwhelmed me, without my knowing why: the rebellious hair on his head and body, the redness of his skin, the wrinkles that seemed to be born in that very instant, on his face, his neck, his arm, his whole body folding into creases as the bloating was gradually reduced.

My sight offered me only a succession of static pictures, my father overcoming metaphors and returning to himself in his usual dimensions, but as I watched him I felt myself witnessing a greater process, life in its slow and weary progression. And also when I locked myself in the bathroom, the only outlet that that space afforded me, I looked at myself in the mirror with astonishment. In my already slightly drooped eyelids I noticed, albeit very attenuated, the same pattern of wrinkles as on my father's eyes. One longer hair on my eyebrow also seemed to evoke his dishevelled brow, and without giving it too much thought I yanked it out as if I were thereby yanking a few years off my age. It wasn't enough. I remember being overtaken at that moment by a dizzying impression, the idea, clearer than ever, that we were both hurtling towards death, and that we would not be able to know each other in time, to understand deeply who we were, who we had been.

I don't know what it is you're looking at the whole time, but I've got something to tell you, something that might ease all that curiosity. His voice was now the deepest he'd been able to speak since his arrival, and I unstuck my back from the armchair in what was merely a reflex of concern, with no idea of what was to come. My paternal grandparents, your great-grandparents, he said, died at Auschwitz. Their names were recorded on a list of 610 Jews persecuted by Nazis in the outskirts of Bistriṭa, in Romania, all of them killed in Auschwitz in 1944. There's no way we can be sure how they died, as you know. It could have been from hunger or a lack of medical care, it could have been exhaustion from the forced labour, but it's unlikely. They were both in their sixties, they were almost certainly condemned on arrival and led directly to the gas chambers.

I returned my back to the armchair, incapable of any response, as if my father's words had plundered all my strength. It shouldn't be shocking, that had always been practically the only thing I'd known about my great-grandparents, that they'd been victims of the Holocaust, that during the war they'd been deported to the camps – to the camps, that was the non-specific term that denoted death. Now, however, the name Auschwitz, with its cultural burden, with its power to evoke a vast gallery of accounts and images, seemed to give the fact an inescapable concreteness. It shouldn't be important, Auschwitz or some other camp, Auschwitz or the battlefield, Auschwitz or a Nazi guard transferring the cruelty of the regime onto his gun, every death was a death in the genocide, absurd and pitiful. Yet all the same, it wasn't sadness or pain I felt, but rather a kind of euphoria, as if this enriched my past, allied me to a great crowd of victims, positioned me in history. Maybe even some pride, the same I'd felt when I learnt of my father's militancy against the dictatorship, but now much less justifiable. What was there for me to take pride in, in circumstances that were so distant, so accidental? Was there any virtue, after all, in the simple condition of being a victim? And why had they wanted to keep this information secret for so long, why hadn't they said?

This last question, unconnected to all my reasoning, was the only one I offered out loud. I only realised I'd said anything when I heard my father's answer: It's never been a secret, Sebastián, it was just a piece of information we were missing. Your grandparents didn't talk about the Holocaust, they didn't research the Holocaust, they didn't exchange information with distant relatives, but it's possible this wasn't a mechanism of repression, but rather the one remaining choice of continuity. They were focused on the present, they wanted to prosper in the country where they'd arrived, your grandfather made hats, his thoughts never escaped anywhere beyond them. As for me, my father went on, I never had that curiosity when I was young, that curiosity you have. For my generation, politics and family, politics and intimacy were never so deeply intertwined. I was much more interested in the collective dimensions, Marxism, socialism, the now lost notion of Zionism with a human face.

There was a serenity in his words, there was no weakness revealed in his tone, his face got lost in the white walls, my father was once again the distracted man who navigated thoughts through the sea of his eyes.

Within that calm, my lightning-flash of euphoria lost any meaning, it was the untimely reaction of a boy's first hearing of a good story. My father, however, seemed to wake from his memory and return to himself and to his circumstances, his body stretched out on a strange bed and a tube draining his lung. It wasn't a secret, he said, it's something I just learned, when I was in Patagonia. Somebody sent me a link to the Holocaust Museum archives, and without giving it much thought I decided to search for my grandparents. That was only a few hours before I started to get short of breath and everything clouded over, and the hard road that brought me to this hospital began.

19.

But there are moments that no pain can invade, there are joys that do not give way to the grief that surrounds them. There are things we live through that become singular, that don't succumb to the greater course of events, that do not allow themselves to be transformed by an ending. There are experiences that retain their place in the memory, untouched since their first moment, inaccessible to words and to thoughts, to any abstraction that might attempt to reinvent them. Some might say these memories lie, that they betray their own history, their subsequent meanings. No. It's words that lie, and thoughts, feelings, abstractions lie: joy, exceptional and illogical, remains true to itself.

I remember she came out of the bathroom, shut the door behind her and came over to sit beside me on the living room sofa. My hand found hers and we interlinked fingers, and in this way we merged palms, joints, nails, for a moment at least we went back to being one single body. Three minutes were required, but the clock had no place in that scene and we remained there for a time that was uncertain, the time of discovery. I think we spent the entirety of the minutes in silence, and it was not an uncomfortable silence, on the contrary, it was the only music that was a match for what we were feeling, for what I believe we felt.

Perhaps we didn't even need to go into that bathroom, to pick up the test from the sink counter, check the result and exchange lightning-flash glances in the mirror. On that sofa, I think we already knew. I could recount the gentleness with which she rested her head on my shoulder, the exact moment when we were seized by the unlikely optimism, the reckless certainty, but it's possible I am merely composing a scene that is fitting for the circumstances. The fact is, to the not very considered beings we knew how to become at that moment, she was already pregnant, we were already starting to gestate that intermediary being, half her, half me, a culmination of the encounter between bodies that had lasted more than a decade. The impression was a strange one, it wasn't a pregnancy test that was waiting for us in the bathroom, it wasn't a declaration of yes or no. It was our child who was waiting for us, occupying a room in our house for the first time.

True happiness is in your own home, among the joys of the family, I remember recalling the statement from Tolstoy, and I remember not dismissing it as I'd done on other occasions, summarily, not challenging its conventional and sentential nature, or the use of such a questionable phrase: true happiness. It was afternoon, we were walking in the shade of the trees of our neighbourhood, we were going together to the clinic to carry out the test that would confirm the result. We were walking lightly, I couldn't feel the friction of the pavement under my feet, I felt we were hovering, close to the ground, at the usual height. Joy is an experience of disconnectedness, I might have thought during the walk, the privilege of distraction in the midst of surrounding pain. Or I never thought about anything because I was myself distracted, because at that moment no guilt could touch me – how could I feel guilt if grief couldn't reach me, if I was unaware of everything else.

At night, once again on the living room sofa, I found myself putting my ear to her belly, as if that tiniest seed that was not so much as a millimetre long could make itself heard, as if it had a discernible existence. It had no face, but it was already not an inexpressive being. It had no name, but it was not as anonymous as it had been the previous night, as it had been for so many months. I enclosed her belly with my hands and felt that I was grasping it. I pressed on her belly and realised it was her I was pressing on while I was fantasising about touching our child, but all the same I didn't want to stop pressing on her. No, I would not abandon this being, I wanted this being always in my hands, and now I no longer knew if I was talking about the child or about her. Let history tread its path of indiscernible meanings and convulsions, I would not be distanced from that moment.

20.

Three times I walked past Demetrio Paiva's open door, three times I didn't go in. He lived on the fourteenth floor, his door immediately opposite the stairs, allowing any passer-by to glimpse a filthy corridor cluttered with things, rolls of fabric, discarded machines. Each time I went past, my legs heavy, chest panting, I saw a man at the end of that corridor as tired as I was, arms hanging limply, shoulders slumped: a man on a wicker stool against the fallow walls of his living room. On other occasions, probably on most occasions, I found his door closed. As I approached, the rhythmic noises of the machines grew louder, the image in my mind gained movement and I would picture him hunched over his work table, focusing on fabrics and needles, and then all this dissipated behind me as I went on climbing step after step.

On the fourth occasion, I no longer wanted that story to dissipate into vague images and I decided to go inside. Demetrio, as I discovered his name was, offered me another wicker stool and a cup of coffee that I didn't know how to refuse. I balanced my recorder on a pile of clothes, pressed the red button and didn't know what to ask. What exactly I intended to hear, what I was doing in his house, was something that eluded us both. Demetrio started to talk about his sewing routine, about the countless hours he spent locked in that room, about the unvarying production of the same shirt, the same trousers, hands tracing the same mechanical marks on the material, the regular intermittent noise of the needles piercing the clothes, the noise that stayed with him even in his hours of rest, even at night, wedged into his immediate memory. All this for a few reals' pay per item, of course, which somebody would sell for a few hundred. He spoke with total indifference, his words likewise mechanical, spoken with no emotion, as though he had sewn those same words too many times before.

His tone only became more inflected when he agreed to reveal a little of his past. He had no origin, he said, he had few memories of the village where he was born, a bunch of mud houses in the outskirts of Cuzco, not far from the centuries-old ruins. It was inevitable that he would escape from there, leave behind his parents and sisters, who wouldn't mind waiting until he had something to bring back. Escaping then became his main job, from Cuzco to Arequipa, from Arequipa to La Paz, and then to the depths of the heights of Potosí, to carve a few miserable grams of silver out of the mud. As this brought him nothing but rough hands, he decided to go down to Asunción, where he now lacked both ceiling and floor. He went on to Ciudad del Este, the city of the east, before this name had yet become so solar, when it was still the grim Puerto Stroessner, a self-tribute by one of those typical tyrants of ours. Escaping from one place to another was now his vital role, crossing the border daily carrying products that some would regard as counterfeits under his arm, exchanging his life for poor pieces of merchandise.

It was only when he realised that the balance would never be in his favour, it was only when he decided that he no longer wanted to carry anything, that he just wanted to pass through, Demetrio alone and his wandering, that a soldier on the border decided not to let him. This was how Brazil welcomed him, with a sudden interruption of his steps, locking him in a stuffy room, not all that different from the one in which we found ourselves, not so different from the way Brazil welcomes him today, each morning and each night, in the unvarying production of the same day. The country didn't have much to offer, the guard laughed: today all he could provide was a laxative and a dozen hours. Not even his body belonged to him, Demetrio felt, or that is what he said he felt. Even the purity of his body was something he needed to prove in the mistrustful eyes of the other man, even his own body had become a piece of unwanted merchandise.

I lost the recorder some time later, on a night I am still keen to talk about. I was also to lose the notebook in which I had scribbled a few of these words, or others, the words that some unknown part of me wanted to erase. But I ask myself, as I imprecisely reconstitute our conversation, whether I ever apologised to Demetrio for the Brazilian soldier's violence, for my country's hostility, or whether I preferred to make use of my own remote origins and join together as his brother, make myself a Latin American, too.

One thing, however, I do remember with total precision. The last statement he made before I got up and held out my hand, perhaps his only true confession. That he might have been unfair when he said he had no origin, that he had no roots. That every day, as he mechanically sewed the same trousers, the same shirt, his thoughts always escape back to the old mud village, to the arms of his parents and sisters, to the centuries-old ruins.

That he doesn't go back home because he is ashamed, of the resounding failure you see in front of you, of this man you see here, whose only achievement in life was to be constantly running away from himself.

21.

They can be worrying, to a would-be father, those first weeks of a pregnancy. Once the euphoria of the discovery has passed, all that remains is an abstract piece of information, the neutral bit of data that a foetus exists – or not even that, that two cells have fused and there's some news of hormones. His wife's body is occupied by a being that will produce nothing but silence, at length, someone who for many months will be almost ethereal. Believing in its existence does not greatly differ from a matter of faith, a certainty founded in uncertain elements, a voluntary surrender to another's doctrine.

I don't know why I'm opting for generalisation here, if I've never heard of the subtle difficulty of this experience from anybody else, if in those days the feeling of an inconsistency of faith was a problem that was exclusively mine – and a problem unspoken, unconfessed, insignificant in any case. Faced with the foetus, faced with her, I had little to say. A good portion of my days was spent in forgetting, and a word or a gesture was needed, some trigger or other, to return me to an awareness of the pregnancy or to belief. And so I went back to fearing that the relationship, established or imminent, would come to be marked by non-communication, that one day I would need to use literature to redeem that ineptitude, too.

To a would-be mother, I imagine the experience of pregnancy might be quite different. What reveals her new state is not a test at the chemist's, it's not the authority of a laboratory with its official report initialled by a doctor. In contrast with its provisional smallness, it produces a myriad of effects, sometimes a start of acid reflux, an inexhaustible tiredness, a persistent hunger. Among the many possible symptoms, sickness is perhaps the most frequent, a constant sea-sickness on dry land. So is this nausea it, this blinding proof? The nausea is him, the nausea is her, the nausea is the foetus.

To her, to the specific mother she was already becoming, that collection of undisputed sensations was the suspension of uncertainty, her emancipation from the domains of belief. She no longer needed to search within herself for the discernible signs, it was no longer the time for her to interrogate her belly, her stomach, her back, and in this way her body recovered the integrity of another time – if not peace, there was harmony between body and mind. The paradox did not elude her: she knew that the tiredness, the hunger, the nausea, that every way of feeling bad was what allowed her to feel good, not to go back to being invaded by the emptiness, by the distressing doubt. The worst moments were the best: when the being that occupied her body made itself so uncomfortable that its presence was undeniable, that yes, its existence was revealed. There was life before birth, and that life was intertwined with hers, it belonged to her like nothing else belonged to her – before it grew, and came detached, and formed itself into another being that was whole, free, independent.

Back in those days only once was I able to share the certainty with her. We woke together that morning, we again took the short walk to the laboratory, less airborne now, more attached to the ground. In a white room with no decoration at all somebody closed us in, turned off the light and turned on the monitor. On the screen vague blotches emerged, an unstable chiaroscuro I didn't know how to decipher, increasingly diffuse images that the specialist illustrated with words, a centimetre-long ellipse in which I was supposed to see my son, my daughter, the head here, the tail that will disappear here, between them the foreshadowing of a spine. Can you both see? An almost obscurantist scepticism still held sway over me and prevented me from saying yes, I saw. That thing was no more than a picture made by a machine, a picture based on unfathomable echoes. It was only the representation of a child, how could I trust that? It was then that the sound passed through the room, a sound I heard without intermediaries, the sound and not its representation, the growing beating of a hurrying heart that became, for a moment, somehow, surprisingly ours.

22.

The kiss I received from my mother on my cheekbone, avoiding my beard, was less dry than the plain meeting of cheeks we practised in the hospital. We were in her house now, in my parents' old house, and the space helped to break through her containment, the coldness with which she insisted on hiding her pain. As long as we didn't talk about my father, she wouldn't need to reveal her impatience with the treatment that was stretching on, that whole month of intensive therapy that was already extrapolating the seriousness of the case, such an excess of care for a man who was solid and healthy. While we were there, her denial could take the shape of pleasant company, of a forgetting of all fatality, of a shared existence in a present stripped of future or past.

We sat at the table, and we were no small number. My father's place remained vacant, as if he might appear at any moment, as if he were once again taking too long to show up for dinner, the stubborn procrastinating that was one of his most deplorable faults. We ate without waiting for him, we ate copiously, arms crossed the table passing dishes, over and over we filled our glasses – and eating like that could only be a return to normality, as if thirst and hunger were measures for our mood. My brother talked about the festival where he'd been working over the weekend, the fire on the ground, the earth burning, did you see it in the photos, such vast amounts of meat, arranged in a circle, feeding the famished multitudes for so many hours. My sister told us about the wedding on Saturday, the party that stretched on till the small hours and the amusing encounter with her analyst when they were both so intoxicated.

We were happy, the family was happy, for the duration of one meal no concern reached us. I thought for a moment that death might be like this, that this is what the loss of our father would be one day, not the severity of the hospital, not the drama of a body going to ruin, being destroyed. Perhaps death is nothing more than this delay in a banal conversation, a feeling of absence amidst the triviality, an underground hurt occasionally surfacing into the hours. Or not quite a hurt, not quite an absence, but an unspoken reminiscence, kept intimately within each of us. But my father was alive, it was no time to be talking or thinking about his death, and perhaps that was why I made the announcement we had agreed to postpone: We've got some good news. It might not look it yet, it might go against all the immediate evidence, but, yes, inside that belly there's a life gestating. And then the cries were full of enthusiasm, and everybody got up and I received a hug from my mother, the kind of hug I no longer remembered, with a caress of my hair, as if she were hugging and caressing the son I'd been three decades before, or a grandchild who was gestating within me.

This is all that should remain of that night, only the memory of joy rising above the pains, silencing the intimate anguishes, the ones we did not announce and that we did not celebrate with toasts. When I was on my way out, however, I noticed a shape behind the curtain, and couldn't contain the impulse to pull the fabric aside. It was a wooden saint beside the window, turned towards the outside, casting its shadow onto the garden. I remembered hearing my mother saying sometimes, in confessions that were always laughable, that she had no problem sustaining her atheism in the easy decades, but that, when the time came, when she was nearing the end, resuming her friendship with the saints of her childhood couldn't hurt.

23.

You want me to tell you about the earthquake, right? Everybody always wants me to tell them about the earthquake, for all Haitians to tell them about the earthquake, said Ginia, in a tone I wasn't able to decipher, a composition carefully pitched between disgust and compliance. Nobody ever wanted to hear from a black woman before, she went on. Now everybody wants to know about our misfortune, about nothing but our misfortune, so long as it's expressed with sensitivity and grief, with the least possible amount of rage. Is that what you want for your book? You want me to lend you my distress, my pain?

Fine, if it's the earthquake you want to know about, I can tell you, I'll give you a few words. It got me when I was starting to go up the stairs in my house, I don't remember for sure what I was fetching from up there. Suddenly, this incredibly powerful boom, and my ears got blocked, my eyes got blocked, I had barely any senses left. The whole building was trembling and, for me, it was reduced to the bannister on the stairs, the only point I was able to hang on to. It was a powerful force coming from below, a bomb imploding the earth from within, that would hurl the whole city into the air. I felt I was being hurled myself, and falling, but falling with my feet firmly planted in the same place, on the second step of the staircase of my house. At this point memory fails me. I don't know how long I was just standing there, far beyond the minute that the quake lasted. When I realised where I was, they were already arriving to pull me out, and it was only then that I opened my eyes. The whole staircase had collapsed, the whole house had collapsed, all that were left were those two steps that saved me. In your book you'll call this luck or chance, I can already tell: I've got another word for it.

It was only when I got outside that I was able to grasp the scale of the disaster. It was only when the screaming overtook the city, screams that came out of everywhere, as if the rubble itself were screaming, as if the whole destroyed city were screaming, in an enormity of voices. Anybody who wasn't screaming merely walked, everybody seemed to be wandering aimlessly down cracked streets. Nothing could be more collective than an event like that, but each one of us lived through it utterly alone. Anybody who saw me might have thought I was wandering aimlessly, but my steps had never been so precise, my hearing was now the keenest of my senses. I was trying to hear the voice of my daughter, to hear her screams coming from somewhere, from the entrails of the earth that was trying to swallow us up. I was still walking in search of my daughter as the city became an open cemetery, with an infinite number of bodies nobody could bury fast enough, which they just piled up with care on the street corners. To this day, so many years later, even so far away, I sometimes catch myself listening to the city, carefully scrutinising the noises, trying to hear the voice I never heard again. Have you got children? Even if my language was not betraying, I mean, even if I am not betrayed by this precarious French that was never my language, I don't know if you'll understand what I mean.

You're really going to put this in your book? Don't stop there, then, say a bit more about Haiti, don't just fall into the whole old story about a sad country, under some mystical curse. You know Haiti's history, you know how the country was formed. Before we existed, our tragedy was already much greater, the greatest disaster ever seen, not a natural catastrophe, but a human catastrophe, colonialism. It was the greatest concentration of slaves on the planet, right there, on our island. And then the rebellion exploded with uncontainable force, the blacks used their everyday tools to destroy the Big House, and those were the only tools that really destroyed it. And so they expelled the exploiters and abolished slavery like it had never been abolished before, not anywhere. Can you imagine how they made us pay for that, how much we're paying still, two centuries later? And yet, not one of us would ever sell our history, the freedom we won by our own strength. We fell, we fall every day, but with our feet firmly planted in the same place. Let the whole earth tremble, those two steps that saved us can never be taken away.

What's your book about? Put something like this, in prettier and correcter words than mine, they can be your words, that's OK. But put something more than pain, something more than misfortune, if you want to write something worth writing.

24.

That morning, said my father, with nothing urging him to speak, as if he had suddenly summoned up the breath to tell the story that was suffocating him, that morning we did the hike through the glacier park. The fields of ice spread out every which way, surrounding us on all sides, obstructing the horizon wherever we looked. The guide was talking non-stop, describing what we could already see, the large blocks in a special colour, the ice that was so compact it swallowed up the white rays, reflecting only that curious blue. You see the hugeness of this solid sea? You feel the smallness of humanity faced with such grandeur? I did feel the smallness of humanity and felt my own body dwindling away, felt as though I was losing the tips of my feet, the fingers of my hands, each extremity frozen.

It was strange, there was no human construction anywhere, no wall to block the view, but even in that vastness the sensation was one of claustrophobia. The beauty of it all was monumental, there was no denying that, so I started to suspect that beauty itself could be claustrophobic, any excessive beauty, a harmony overpowering us, oppressing us with its impeccable presence. This is eternal ice, the guide explained, which has existed since long before the appearance of humanity, as eternal as the mountains, as the lakes, as God. And yet, the ice is melting from human action, you see the irony? I could see mountains, I could see the lake, and if by chance, affected by that little man's superlative tone, I were to see God, it would be a God melting before my very eyes, the water making its way down the glaciers, wrinkles that seemed to be born in that very moment on that vast blue face.

When I left that place, it was with regret and relief. We returned to El Calafate in search of a restaurant, but I couldn't decide, I couldn't stop anywhere, I could have kept on walking forever around those tourist alleyways. Your mother ran out of patience and decided the whole thing was ridiculous, that we'd eat at the hotel, but I sensed that I wouldn't feel too good between walls and positioned myself on the balcony of our room, still fearful of claustrophobia, of the distress from before, the persistent nausea. And then, beneath the limpid sky, that link with no context, that page in Hebrew that cast me back into my childhood, the interminable archive of documents and the grandparents I never knew, the 610 from Bistrița and Auschwitz and all the stuff I've already told you.

I think it was only then that I started to understand what I'd been feeling on the glaciers, the cosmic terror, as Bakhtin called it, the fear that ravages us when we think we're faced with the immeasurable, with the unknowable. The fear upon which almost all religion's based, forged by a God who is oppressive and protective all at once. The fear that almost all fascism takes advantage of, too, the fear of something uncertain, mythical, an enemy erected and sculpted with great care, and most conveniently, Jewish, immigrant, socialist, black, female, homosexual, militant, marginalised. All this became ordered in my mind with a tremendous clarity, as limpid as the sky that covered me, even if I can't seem to be clear at all, I know, and I'm sorry, in what I'm telling you now.

25.

It was evening, I was still alone on the hotel balcony, when I felt all that anguish and all that nausea converging towards my chest. Up until that moment I hadn't realised I was short of breath, I thought I was overcome by a metaphysical ailment, or by the displeasure of bad news and unhappy thoughts. Then came the shortness of breath, strikingly present. A distant feeling of asphyxiation might perhaps have been with me since the start of the morning, subterraneous, beneath every movement, but now it was shocking, manifest. Suddenly I was no longer able to breathe, and to breathe, the most natural of acts, became a conscious imperative. I needed to breathe, I needed to remember to breathe, not run the risk of forgetting to breathe, fulfilling my obligation to breathe, catering to my desire to breathe. Inhale as much air as I could and exhale as much air as I could.

When the ambulance came to my aid, when the paramedic asked what kind of pain I was feeling, I said the pain in my thorax was strong, but the pain was even stronger in my shoulder muscles from the effort of breathing. Your mother was looking at me in astonishment, she was holding my hand as though my survival depended on it, as if I were a man shipwrecked and with the mere strength of her fingers I could not drown in the sea. I didn't understand this because metaphors were of no use to me, no thought that took me away from what was most fundamental to me. My whole existence seemed to depend on a literality, that my lung fulfil the function of a lung and process the air, that my heart fulfil the function of a heart and pump the air, that my mouth do without language and limit itself to taking in and expelling the air.

What happened next I think you already know, that was the desperation that reverberated to where we are now, your mother's incessant calls to the doctors, to her children, to anybody who might get us out of that torment. We kept going, however, further and further south, we immersed ourselves in southernness, in the deepest continent. In the hospital at Río Gallegos, a young doctor wanted to save me by pumping gusts of air into my mouth, which would have destroyed me within minutes. Another reckless doctor punctured my lung when he tried to insert the drain, and I started to blow up until I became the grotesque creature you met. For many long hours I was an inert, impassive body, bouncing from one place to another, pushed to the medical plane and then returned to the emergency room, with nobody able to decide whether it was safe to leave, whether that group of organs in critical condition would make it through the journey.

I was stripped of myself, I didn't exist except as a being going into imminent failure. And then I decided that this was not enough, that breathing couldn't be an end in itself, something so bland and irrelevant, so lacking in pleasure. I needed to live, I needed to remember to live, not run the risk of forgetting to live, fulfilling my obligation to live, catering to my desire to live. Inhale as much life as I could and, only later, when the time came, exhale all my life at once. And that was what brought me here, wanting to see all of you, wanting to see the world despite everything, wanting to see everything that exists and everything that is yet to exist.

Dad, I'm going to have a child.

That's such lovely news, Julián. Thank you for telling me.

No, dad, thank you. But here you've got to call me Sebastián.

26.

Najati was waiting for me at the door, he didn't want me to come inside. He wanted to escape from those walls that were so close, from that claustrophobic space he refused to call his home, he wanted to walk. The city, he said, was gradually becoming more domestic than those scant square metres in which each morning he found himself confined. This wasn't his city, São Paulo was nothing like Homs, their streets and their trees so different, but there's something about co-existing on the sidewalks that makes everyone the same, he said, that makes us all, for a few brief steps, just people with no origins, with no histories, fellow dwellers in a single present that is everything even if it doesn't last at all. In this way I forget myself for a moment, I forget my loved ones and I make myself into another.

For a long time, however, Najati's walking was restricted to precise limits, a coming and going along the same sidewalk without ever crossing a street, turning around each time he came to a traffic light, whether it was green or red. I followed at his side, not daring to say anything, and the strangeness of it pushed me away from his speech, distracted me from the afflictions he was confiding to me. He was saying something about the difficulty of making contact with his family, it had been weeks since he'd spoken to Sumayya, and his wife, still in Syria, had become entirely inaccessible. He was saying something about the crazy desire to return, to see his land albeit in ruins. His plan was failing, it now seemed very unlikely that they would be together again anywhere, that I do remember him saying, and I remember thinking I understood that his way of walking was all down to nerves, as if he were oscillating back and forth, unable to resolve an impasse.

I was still attentively observing his steps, I was still trying to find some way of showing my solidarity, when Najati finally stopped at a traffic light, waited for it to change, and we crossed over to the other side. From then, as we walked with no more boundaries, the conversation turned freer and sunny. Not long before, I had asked him what it was that had, finally, brought him to Brazil, and now he talked about the role of chance in personal journeys, about sudden decisions, about unexpected meetings. Perhaps Brazil had been the wrong choice, he said, especially given the direction things had taken, but he was happy, if it's possible to say such a thing, to be a part of a new community, and a community engaged in a struggle against the folly governing us everywhere. There's something I've been able to understand here, he went on, that although oppression might spill from country to country, conquering entire continents, resistance too is expansive, it too crosses borders.

In the occupation they insist that we are a family, a family of refugees in our own land or in a foreign one, and at first I found that strange, said Najati. Then I thought there could be no more exact definition. Yes, because the world is made up of infinite transits between places, of the continuous movement of beings. Like my family, every family has, if we go far enough back in time, countless displacements in its origin. All humanity is made up of this incessant movement, and it only exists in the way we know it thanks to these displacements. Deep down – I was listening now with absolute concentration – deep down, if we go far enough back in time, we reach the most obvious conclusion of all: that each one of us has travelled their own path, but that we are all descendants of the same absolute distant ancestor, and that, therefore, however different we may be, we are all part of one and the same family.

It might seem like it is, but this is not an uplifting sort of comment, Najati made a point of clarifying. This reasoning has two rather troubling consequences. First, that all love has something incestuous about it, it will always be a love between siblings or between cousins. Second, and perhaps more important, the idea that, if we're part of the same immense family, any violence against the other is a violence against ourselves, doomed to destroy each of us and all humanity in one go.

Once again I didn't know what to say, I just felt a kinship stronger than ever with this man who was so different from me, I felt our co-existence there on the pavement made us equals, even without eliminating our origins and our histories. It was only when we started to walk back up the steps of the Cambridge, at his slow and heavy pace, that I decided to comment on the potency of his words, whether spoken or written, I decided to suggest we look for some place to publish them. He didn't even stop walking to dismiss the possibility: don't waste your time, I'm not remotely interested in literature. I'm only interested in an opening for dialogue.

27.

As I was already leaving, a silent figure stepped into my way, and it took me a moment to recognise the stern face of Carmen. She asked me to accompany her into her room, we needed to talk. Sitting opposite that woman, with the door she'd locked behind me, I felt an urgent need to know her in some intimate way, to hear something real about her past, about her history. Something more than the categorical words she shouted in the assemblies, her voice wavering, always creating a feeling somewhere between astonishment and enthusiasm. But in that moment, in me, perhaps there was only astonishment, and so I found myself paralysed, unable to find the questions that might open a way to the confidence I desired.

You're a writer, that much I know already. I also know you've spent some days in the little room up on the fifteenth, that's more serious. But you needn't worry, I'm not bothered, that's not why I've asked you in. The room's unoccupied, you can take refuge there for as many hours as you think you need. I don't know what you're running away from, what fear or sadness is making you want to isolate yourself in such a precarious space, but fine, it's nothing to do with me, and I genuinely don't mind. Everybody here always seems to be running away from something, you're welcome to add your flight to ours.

That woman with her brusque gestures and categorical phrases, I realised, was somebody I would never dare to ask a personal question: to her, any exploration of memory must seem futile. Her history would be a void, a gap that nothing could remedy, I was already starting to feel sorry, but her words cut through my regret and returned me to the concreteness of the room. I know you've spoken to some of the residents, I know you've been trying to understand who they are, what they do, what brought them to the occupation. Do whatever you like, talk to whoever you want, that's your right. But you should know it's useless. If you want to understand this place, best to forget about the personal journeys, the private lives. If you want to understand this place, best not to lose sight of the collective, best join us in the struggle. Come round to the party on Sunday, come well rested, bring something to eat and a few items of clothing.

28.

I try to remember the moment when she once again allowed herself to be overtaken by the uncertainty, the precise instant in which her fullness broke. I think we were in the car, headed down a slow road, when she mentioned she hadn't felt anything in her body for a while, or rather, yes, she did feel something unusual, the beginnings of a pain in her belly, still subtle, inconsistent. It's probably nothing, the uterus expanding is bound to cause some discomfort, I might have said to calm her, and she agreed with no particular emphasis while still insisting that there was something strange about the discomfort, about the now intermittent nausea, almost a restlessness of her insides. It's probably nothing, now she was the one saying it, trying to calm me down or to bring the conversation to a close, must be the stress of the journey, or the anxiety about the days ahead.

Maybe the trip hadn't been a good idea, those first months of pregnancy are fragile, the doctor had said, but nonetheless we kept on going, we joined dozens of our friends, managed to borrow a car, bought tickets for the boat, and on the isolated peninsula we rented a fishing hut. Those days were the last of the year, and this had always been our way of celebrating, seeking out the ocean to relax our bodies and stretch out our gaze, which had been atrophied all year by the city. Thus we played at completing a cycle. Sometimes we agreed we weren't really bothered about the arbitrariness of the date, that the ritual was worth it for its own sake, for our wish to compensate in languor for the apparent efforts we had been building up. And so we would make that night into a unique night, not because the calendar so determined it, but because on that night we would be unavoidably together, drunk, eager, excited, until the first rays of sunlight soothed us.

On those days, surrounded by friends, assailed by that almost compulsory joy, we had no choice but to simulate the enthusiasm we were lacking. She would not speak of the subject again, she would smile each time somebody's toast included the new life we were creating, but I felt that something had split in her tranquillity. I would hold her hand, interweaving my fingers in hers, but it was as if they lacked heat and flesh, her fingers were no more than thin bones wrapped in flaccid skin. I could not touch her, could not gain access to her pain or her distress, her insecurity or her fear. I hugged her and could not contain her, once again her existence escaped me. And the silence she insisted on extending only aggravated my impression that there was something wrong, something we were not yet allowing ourselves to name. The days went by and the feeling grew that we were living through something monstrous, albeit so small and personal, we were living through Schrödinger's pregnancy: like the cat the scientist had imagined inside a box, with its future and present uncertain, inside her body there might be a living child or a dead child, a *living-dead* child, a being suspended in time that no amount of will might save.

Shortly before midnight, she took my hand, pulling me away from the party that was already bubbling up around us. I couldn't tell whether what I saw in her eyes was sadness or terror, and I might have lowered my gaze when she told me about the stain that had appeared again, red now, sinister like never before. We sat on the sand and there we stayed, shoulders stuck together in a single shared muteness, with no interest in the customary denial, until we were surrounded by the euphoric groups who were getting ready to count down the seconds to the moment clocks would strike twelve.

I think we got up to escape that, and we walked down to the sea for want of any other destination. Jumping seven waves was one of the few superstitions we allowed ourselves, not out of any belief in its power, as we admitted to ourselves, but for the opportunity to name our longings, to give some order to our ambitions and desires. I looked at the sea now, unending in that black pitch, and I could name only fear. A few metres behind her, I gave up on jumping the illuminated strand of foam when I saw that she was not jumping, that she was paralysed, just allowing the waves to wash her feet and bury her ever deeper in the sand. Perhaps at that moment she had just one single desire, an obvious and domineering one, already known to be past, which the strength of the waves could only dissolve.

29.

We did not remain on the beach until the sun soothed us, we didn't believe it would soothe us this time. We fled the party without telling anyone, we retired to the bed with the creaky springs. The house didn't have electricity, and in the darkness nobody would know our sadness, we ourselves would not be able to confirm our own dejection in each other's face. We went to sleep as soon as we could, or I went to sleep and persuaded myself that she was sleeping beside me. It wasn't long before I felt her hand on my shoulder, rigid now, with no tenderness, only tension, pulling me to follow her to the bathroom. She had bled again, and this time it was not only the red stickiness, there seemed to be something denser, something thicker. I followed the focus of her flashlight until it lit up the murky water, and there, at a glance, almost submerged, a piece of torn fabric, an egg of imprecise outlines and greyish in tone. The ghostly body that would come to inhabit her nightmares, and which I would banish from mine.

Under the heavy rain that took hold of the sky the following day, on the only corner of the beach where the phone could pick up a signal, we discovered that we needed to leave, right now, with real urgency. But no boats would be going in such angry weather, let alone on the first day of the year, and so we walked slowly back along alleyways and staircases to the darkness of the house and collapsed one last time onto the mattress with the creaky springs. Of those empty hours, of that night of waiting and recurrence, I remember not one word, not one gesture.

I remember that a boat finally took us across to the car, it was January 2nd, and that we there began the longest journey we had ever made, even if history does not confirm the fact. On the single-lane road, it was as if every car were in mourning, inert, unmovable. We could be in that Cortázar story now, the one we had once read together, out loud, we could be trapped in infinite traffic, counting finite days, inventing relationships in the midst of the paralysis, but all of that was too real for surrealism to be able to describe. Inside that car, there was my body and hers, without any fictions to abduct us. Inside the car, there was above all her body in its physical dimension, and another body she no longer contained, and in my body, in an imperceptible shiver, a vague fear that hers might be submerged beneath the murky water, too. She kept saying we were never going to get there, this traffic was insurmountable, and perhaps it was to keep my own fear at bay that I became impatient, that I condemned her foolishness harshly. I think she stopped hearing me after this, and we spent the thirteen hours of the journey in a silence made up of just any old words.

It was very early in the morning when we arrived at the hospital, my father must have been asleep and it wouldn't even have occurred to me to go and find him on this occasion. After so many days being afraid that a sadness was going to be inaugurated there, in that place, I was now the one bringing my own sadness, I was the person who was bringing a death, albeit such a discreet one. Or might that not be the correct term? The on-call obstetrician didn't take long to appear, to explain that there was no longer anything visible on the ultrasound, no remains of the foetus, the cervix already closed up, it was a complete spontaneous abortion. It's good news, that was what he thought to say, and lacking any other ideas, or out of mere tiredness after so many unsettled days, and I'm not sure why I'm even justifying myself here, I turned towards her myself and repeated: It's good news. This became the conclusion of the official version that we would soon tell our family, our friends. When she said it, when she insisted on the phrase that was the doctor's and that was mine, even if nobody might notice it, I always heard the veiled irony, the unacknowledged hurt, the accusation she would never make.

30.

In the days that followed, in the weeks, in the months, the house became vast like it had never been before, missing one inhabitant. And yet there was no longer any extra space, every little corner was necessary in order for us to keep our distance, every wall protected us from possible thoughtless words, possible insensitive looks. She went to bed earlier and earlier, she woke up earlier and earlier. I went to bed and woke up later and later, and we sometimes even passed each other in the small hours. I would go into the bedroom and find her curled up, hugging her knees under the sheet, I don't want to say in a foetal position, but it was an unusual pose for her, in more than ten years I'd never seen her sleep like that before. When I lay down beside her, I always felt some movement, she might accommodate her back against my ribs, and for a few moments we would be redeemed by touch, but the moments passed and we were no longer close, back and ribs no longer fitting perfectly together.

I wanted to tell her not to be like this, that it didn't have to be so sad. That there was no reason to lose sleep, that it wasn't worth the tears that she held back or hid, from me or from herself. I wanted to tell her we were young, yes, we'd proved ourselves able to engender one life, that it wouldn't take us long to engender another, and who knows, maybe another after that, if the right moment came along. I think I said this several times, and other times she must have said things that were similar, but words were of little use to us now, they were empty conventions, conveniences that produced no more than the briefest burst of strength. And any word, any idea, any act, any gesture could provoke misunderstandings, which could provoke discussions, which could provoke disagreements. Our dictionary, our encyclopaedia, our anthology, our atlas, everything had aged from one moment to the next, everything had been forgotten, the pages all untouched, yellowed, covered in dust. Perhaps we had become illiterate in the language of our intimacy.

One day she bought a hammock, the one she had promised in a dream to our non-existent daughter. I put it up in the living room myself, rather clumsily, unskilled with domestic tools, and during the attempt we broke into the laughter of the awkward. But it didn't seem safe for us to lie in it together, the weight might be excessive, so it was she who lay down and gave her shape to the material, and it was a long time before she came out again. It was a wide hammock, with red stripes, it enveloped her whole body, in every respect it resembled a cocoon. With her there, shut up in the hammock, the apartment was emptied of any other person's gaze, and its vastness, its solitude, became more oppressive than ever.

It was around that time that I received the call from Najati, his hoarse voice cutting through our muteness, his unusual question about exiles and lives adrift, the strange conversation I have recounted already. I think I would have taken any opportunity to get out of the house, on that day and in the days that followed, in the weeks, in the months.

31.

And then there was no longer any high-pitched quality to his voice, the high-pitched sounds overtaking the room were others, violins and flutes and assorted instruments, a lively melody that defied the hospital's sanitary morbidity. Amid that ordered gibberish, it took me a while to locate my father, to rule out his presence among the rumpled sheets, to spot him in the armchair where I usually sat. My father with his head raised and lips wide, soaking up a profound pleasure from the music, soaking up the world with closed eyes. My father as I never thought to see him again, abstracted from any pain that might still be in his body, distracted from any end that might be approaching. I didn't want to betray his pleasure right away and so I remained silent, motionless as I watched his motionlessness, which was broken only by the swaying of his hand that conducted the air. What's this, dad, I asked at last, where has this unexpected peace come from? And the reply, an evasive one, sounded like an invitation for me also to forget the finiteness of life, this piece, it's Bach, from *Brandenburg Concerto No. 2*, and to accept for a moment the infiniteness of art.

That morning we didn't say anything else and it didn't feel as though anything was lacking. There was nothing to say now, no confession to make, no redemption summoning us – perhaps now, like us, words would be able to rest. I also didn't need the uncomfortable protection of my phone, I didn't want to be made murky by increasingly deplorable news, or to make use of a book that might steal me away from where I was, right there and then. That morning, once the initial surprise had passed, looking at my father or not looking at him was all the same, he would be there by my side, he would still be my father with his same hands and his same arms, strong or weak. He would be my father without a segmentable body that it was my lot to describe, that it was my lot to find strange.

The morning ended with the arrival of lunch, which he rejected with an obvious expression of disgust. The music became more dramatic, it must have been the climax of some sonata, and I couldn't help but reproach him: it was important that he have food, hunger could exacerbate his weakness, he should at least have some of the meat. My father waited for the nurse to leave the room. I'm tired, he said, I can't stand any more of this bland hospital food. But, yes, I'll follow that fatherly advice of yours, I'll have the meat, a nice piece of meat. I've asked your brother to bypass the regulations today, to bring me a rib-eye steak with grilled potatoes, he should be arriving any minute.

I wondered whether that might be a last request, a request from a man condemned to die who has been granted a final meal. No. It didn't take me long to notice how excessive that metaphor was and to see the drama that I had living within me, the drama that was nowhere to be seen in that body, in that room, the drama that the music was no longer evoking, with its subtle and delicate melody. My father was alive, all the risk had become inertia, he was out of danger, my father was not a condemned man. And then, as soon as I granted myself permission to dismiss it, I felt death becoming a crude impossibility, a piece of utter nonsense that could only have been invented by the darkest of minds. That a body should exist there, whole and lively, and in the next second be interrupted, stilled, no longer reacting, no longer waking, passing wordlessly into non-existence. How could something so ludicrous happen, and how could it be so common, so accepted everywhere?

32.

And then there was no longer any high-pitched quality to her voice, Carmen's voice was as sombre as her face, but her words did not reflect this gravity. Carmen talked with sober enthusiasm about the party that would be starting that night, about a communion of forces, about the trajectories that were flowing together now, and in the next few hours, in confluence towards the same point. And it's not just any point, you'll see, it's somewhere wonderful, it can shelter so many of us and many others, it can be the reward after all the injustice, all the pain. With each sentence I felt the euphoria in the lobby growing, I watched arms almost raised, shouts contained, all the imminence of movements announced in the vibrating of the bodies. But of course nothing is guaranteed, Carmen's tone changed, nothing is won by merely deciding, today's conquest will require a great deal of resolve, a great deal of effort. That's how it goes, we know it: you struggle or you die. And then she repeated the words, her voice high-pitched again, now in a shout, you struggle, and everybody released themselves from their containment to complete the line in chorus, or you die!

There must have been three hundred of us, three hundred and fifty, who left a few minutes later, piercing the silence of the night, taking to the street with daring steps. To almost all of us, the destination was unknown: walking was our first mission, pace our feet to our neighbour's, keep moving ahead without knowing where to. The fact that we were going against the traffic, up the road, that we were marching while everyone else was withdrawing, was something that enlivened us, an unacknowledged guarantee. Awaking when so many people were allowing themselves to be overtaken by sleep, by the torpor of a negligible Sunday: the good sense of waking already slipping inside. Opposition was the only thing that could make sense in a present in such disarray. Only disorder was reasonable faced with the unreason of order.

We hadn't got far from the Cambridge when the march rushed towards a specific point, a door that opened in a high outer wall to reveal the most sombre façade ever. The abrupt movement changed the mood of the moment, it broke the delicate harmony of the collective, broke the fragile integrity of its bodies. Quick, quick, somebody said, and legs hurried through. Quick, the voice insisted, and our eyes were no longer able to contemplate that gloomy building. Stripped of the collective, I lost the shamelessness of the plural, I existed in myself alone, listening to the tension in the voices, looking at the apprehensive faces. In some of those faces, apprehension went so far as to take on the features of fear, and in them I no longer saw neighbours, that fear was something I could not be a part of, it was a fear I could not share.

At the top of the building, a dozen floors up or so, somebody had already affixed a flag: a piece of red fabric that was lifeless, wretched in the absence of any wind, a reflection of the wretchedness of the building itself. It took me some time looking at the flag before I could make out the symbol of the FLM, the Housing Struggle Movement, it took me some time to realise that we were crossing over from the imaginary of marching to the symbolism of war. Behind me, a few men were already starting to build a barricade, piling up branches, stones, bricks, any heavy debris they could find, they were already covering the whole door. They were following the orders of an imposing-looking woman, who was stationed by the wall, a woman with strong arms and huge hair – it was only when I registered that detail that I recognised the figure of Preta, the young woman with the animated, happy eyes whom I'd heard speak at the first meeting I attended.

For over an hour that door would be the centre of attention, surrounded by so many watchful eyes. On the other side, the police were assembling vehicles, positioning their men, using loudspeakers to spread their threatening clichés. They didn't sound very convincing: there was impatience in that mechanical voice, some kind of dissatisfaction with the mission it had been assigned by its superiors. In that door a whole universe of class struggles and tensions might have been condensed, I thought for a moment, the inevitable confrontation between the dispossessed and the guardians of property, I went on, but I soon dropped the jargon. What was much more expressive was the language of abandonment, the actual thing that was being fought over: a building that was an invalid, dead, nothing but an empty carcass. The flag nailed over the ruined building was a testament to irrationality.

When the battle for the door seemed to be over, when the police had given up on using its unreasonable force, I saw Preta turn her back on the men and move away. Everything was dark, everything was inhospitable, but for several long minutes she wandered between the dry trees of the surrounding plot of land, deftly skirting around debris and roots, with the utmost mastery of the ground on which she trod. When she reached a mulberry tree with leaves that were still green, she leant back on it, stretched out an arm and started to eat mulberries. In that context, eating mulberries seemed so unusual that my surprise became conspicuous, and when she came back she addressed a few words to me.

You don't get it, do you? You think all this effort is for nothing, for a dirty plot of land, for a building that's falling to pieces. You don't know what this place was like the first time we occupied it, you don't know this was the house of life itself incarnate. I was a child, you can't imagine how many memories I've got of this place, how many nights I come back to this garden, not in shadows like this, to a garden that is bathed in sun. Those dreams never show the misfortunes, the day they took all the families out, without any of the threats like they're making today, with the notorious promise to transform everything into low-income housing – the day when life ended up under the flyover. My mother is doing the right thing, Carmen's doing the right thing, not to give up on this place. Promises or threats, it's those men who choose their weapons: our weapons, our bodies, will always be more vital.

33.

Two spacious halls sheltered our small crowd. When I went inside, still buzzing from the previous hour's commotion, I found almost everybody lying down, calm, weaving a night of rest. Thin, uneven sleeping mats had invaded every bit of space, receiving a mass of similarly uneven bodies. The smaller bodies of the children, far more numerous than I had noticed on our walk, already echoed with a deep sleep, almost implausible in that setting. Maybe so as not to disturb them, the previously raised voices were now no more than whispers, reticent confessions, sighs that evoked a story that was vaster than I was able to follow.

Beside me, in the empty corner where I had curled up, I heard two women talking. The first, her body shielding three or four intertwined children, was describing nights of insomnia in municipal shelters, the rigidity of their rules, the contempt of the staff, the many humiliations endured for a bed and a precarious roof. So true, it's so like that, I know what it's like, the other would agree at the end of each sentence, beating her fist into the palm of her hand. I lived for years in the master and mistress's house, I mean, in the little corner of their house where they confined me, in those slave-quarters two metres square. Every night they'd wake me up, repeating my name as if they were praying, like I was the family's religion. They wanted a tea, they wanted me to check if there was anybody outside, they wanted their glasses of champagne or of cognac. One night, a month ago now, I was so used to it that I just woke up on my own, and I realised they weren't there. I decided to leave, I went to gather up my belongings and I realised there was almost nothing. I carried on gathering other things, the teapot, the glasses, even some bottles, I took whatever I could, I stole for the first time in my life, I stole feeling no shame about stealing. My friend, the first woman responded when the other woman lowered her eyes, ashamed: they were the ones who took everything from you, they were the ones who stole your hands, your eyes, and if you'd let them they would even have stolen your voice.

I don't know why I got up at that moment, ashamed – as if I were a witness, an accomplice, guilty of the crime they were reporting. No one was judging me, there was no contempt in the eyes that looked at me, but the ridiculousness of my presence in that room seemed so evident, taking possession of a vacant corner that somebody else could be occupying, taking possession of other even more vacant corners. I, an onlooker, an intruder, a mole. I, a looter of stories, stealing from these people, their eyes, their hands, even their voice. I think that was where I left my recorder behind, as if by doing that I might get rid of the evidence incriminating me. Now I was crossing the crammed space dodging bodies and thoughts, trying to free myself from the sudden discomfort, from the distress or the nausea, from that unnameable something that was converging towards my chest. From another corner, hugging his legs and leaning on the wall, even more curled up than I had been, Demetrio Paiva threw me a quick wave, which I certainly didn't know how to accept.

I left the room not knowing where to go, the door to the streets still blocked, I couldn't leave even if I wanted to. Instead I went further into the building, down a gloomy corridor, immersing myself in southernness, I thought, immersing myself in the depths of the centre. I crossed through a vastness of new rooms, identical to the first, lit only by the glare of the city coming in at the windows, which no longer had glass now, frames, jambs, mere open holes. In the smaller rooms, old bathrooms, not one mirror was left, not one toilet bowl or tile, not even the pipes remained, yanked off the walls. I went up the stairs noticing the scale of the looting, the worn granite of the steps, split by blows from the tools of despair.

The morphology of the remains was expressive, ordered as it was by the syntax of time. Over that building's skeleton, dissolving into dust now, the spoils of a more recent battle were still spread: worm-eaten mattresses, odd shoes in the corners, needles and syringes, piles of well-worn clothes, tools and old objects, destitute leftovers of the world. Perhaps that wreckage did not tell the entire story of that space over the decades, of what had been a government department with its offices and its waiting rooms, and was once abandoned, of what was the first occupation by organised inhabitants, and was again abandoned, of what was then the arrival of beings who were even more destitute, even more squalid, who had been plundered of everything, on a hunt for any value that might save them, that might guarantee them one more day of existence. But yes, that wreckage in its blunt grammar, I thought somewhere between impressed and melancholic, it did tell of the endless successions of mistakes that led to the total debacle, the story of our civilisational failure.

That was a ruin, nothing else I'd seen before deserved that name. That was a ruin and it seemed to hide in its debris all the ruins that came before, as if from the whole world only a single ruin could remain, I thought, just one trail of destruction spreading infinitely.

It was almost an hour before I started to notice the inscriptions, the letters scrawled on the walls, even more accurate relics of the life that had not ceased to exist in the run-down building. Everywhere I could read names, so many occupiers obsessed with recording their presence, with declaring that one night, whenever it was, they'd been there, they'd suffered there. Everywhere I read names as though by doing so I could pay them some respect, show my pity for the victims, just as I had once done before the wall of those who had been transported to the camps, or the disappeared in Latin America. But now I had no name to look for here, none of my people had suffered in this building, these names were all unknown to me. And I learnt then that I could not exempt myself, that I could not ally myself to the multitude of victims, and once again I felt the anguish or the nausea, the unnameable thing that was flowing towards my chest, much more intense. I felt there was no place in me for euphoria or sadness, there was place only for horror.

34.

I didn't sleep that night. I don't know how long I spent walking among the debris, my gaze moving between the illuminated city and that little corner of darkness. Dawn was breaking, a white light was beginning to wash each shadow, when I could no longer feel my legs and I collapsed in the first hall. Though not everybody was asleep, a new silence hovered, it was thicker, a silence that went beyond sleep or haziness, similar enough to the slightest peace.

And then the silence was ousted by a noisy waking. From all sides bodies were being reborn, much more vigorous than I could have imagined, or than their rest had proclaimed. It wasn't long before those unequal torsos were once again forming an indistinct crowd, it wasn't long before arms and legs were becoming noticeable, and backs that began to carry far away everything that I had insisted on lamenting. Still sprawled in one corner, still motionless, I watched the moving of the wreckage, already freed of its more sensitive weight, of its metaphorical power: a ragged sofa, the frame of a stove, a broken chair, all kinds of unusable objects and nothing more. From the outside, next to the garden, a pile of debris was growing at astonishing speed, in less than an hour it had grown to several metres in height. And now I was imagining each room of the building freed from those burdens, each space stripped of its painful past, free to welcome new women and new men.

I got up and began to wander. I saw Demetrio sweeping a patio, silent and solitary, or merely focused. Najati I didn't see anywhere. Some floors up, I could make out Rosa among a group of people who were improvising a hoist, to remove the larger pieces of furniture through the window. None of them would themselves be moving to the new occupation, I knew that, none of them would be abandoning the rooms that housed them at the Cambridge, the meagre spaces that they distractedly already called home. This was an act of solidarity, I understood, a movement that conceived and prepared a home for other people, for those who perhaps lacked the necessary energy themselves. I would not be abandoning my home either, and I felt energised at that moment, taking up in my arms a hollow door that had been dumped on the ground, contributing with what strength I still had. The door blocked most of my line of sight as I came down the stairs, but that didn't bother me, I trusted that the step would be there, even if it was faulty, even if it was corroded, I trusted in the next step. I would not be abandoning my home either, I would not be abandoning the child I didn't have, I wouldn't be abandoning her.

That day and in the days that followed, in the weeks, in the months, I would come to understand something about what I was looking for there, the reason I escaped so many times to the same place, to the homeless residents' occupation. The calls they made, the book I would write, everything was an excuse for me to take shelter from the ruined present, to allow myself to be seized by an unlikely burst of strength. Occupying was an imperative for all those people, occupying the squares, the streets, the empty buildings, populating them with their still solid bodies, with their uncontainable lives. Occupying was a matter of urgency for bodies, converted into the bluntest of political acts, confronting the resignation of those who are more serene. Occupying, even if it was in order to be among many, to exist yet again as part of the collective. My own imperative might have been a different, albeit impossible one: to turn myself into a square, to turn myself into a street, to turn myself into an empty building, so that whatever's uncontainable about life might come to occupy me at last.

35.

Mia, my dear friend,

You know how lonely it is to be an author facing his own book. There are some people who feel like the characters are with them, that the painfully chosen words cover their silence, that future readers exist. I feel nothing but this exile on the other side of the page, this voluntary exile, this intimate desert. Every sentence is an attempt to cross the border, an attempt that is disastrous, that is frustrated as it was on other occasions. So I am writing to you as if I were writing my book, so that we might share some of the loneliness, knowing that we cannot share each other's company.

It's already been a while since we were last together, in tangible reality, in the actual concreteness of the world, with a table between us, generously laden with food, with papers, with drink. I told you about the book I was starting to write, about my desire to expand, to go beyond my own petty dramas. To go beyond those beloved people surrounding me, too, to examine others and contemplate their abysses – was it you who wrote something like that? The eyes of others, that was my original title, presumptuous, I can see now, in supposing that I would be able to see them, to face them head-on. You were as generous as ever, you didn't want to call out my presumption, remember? You said I should try, I should look into the eyes of others to seek something other than my own reflection, I should dive into the eyes of others until I lose myself.

This is what I have, this thing I'm sending you now, these hundred or so pages in slim chapters. I don't think I have managed to lose myself, in every word that I've attributed to others I've found a word of my own, in every house of somebody else's I have rummaged through mine, in every face I've recognised my face, out of addiction, out of stubbornness. If I wanted to get closer to others, if I wanted to understand them, perhaps I've failed miserably. Even those who are close to me, even my father, even my wife, have become strangers: I barely understand what they say to me in these pages, I don't know what to say to them, I cannot even name them, or hug them. More unfathomable still are the occupiers of this book, though they do not lack names: Najati, Rosa, Demetrio, Ginia. They tell me their stories, they say such powerful things that sometimes they cloud my senses and I no longer know how much I'm taking in, and above all I don't know what to give back, how to repay them.

All I do is allow them to occupy me, to occupy my writing: an occupied literature is what I can do at this moment. And this, in a final movement, is how I find myself lost – but not in the liberating sense you professed that day. My occupiers lead me outside my own domains, and I'm no longer certain where I'm going. I'm writing a book about fatherhood without being able to become a father – and probing motherhood as if I didn't know that I will never learn it. I'm writing a book about death without ever having felt it switch off a body, in a speculation of feelings that one day will seem laughable, when I do encounter the pain. I'm writing a book about the pain of the world, the poverty, exile, despair, rage, tragedy, ludicrousness, a book about this interminable ruin surrounding us, which so often goes unnoticed, but as I write it I am protected by solid walls.

Perhaps you can't recognise the smiling fellow I was back then in these pessimistic words. This is a time for few smiles in this country, and there are days when so many people's dismay infects us. There is one character I have not mentioned here, who at first sight may seem secondary, but who at this moment occupies my entire existence, albeit discreetly, surreptitious. Preta was arrested. She's been detained for several months now, on some vague anonymous accusation, some convenient lie. Preta is being detained because her name means Black, because she has that huge hair, she's the one who says as much. I've just watched an interview she gave in prison, I've watched it several times in a row, and now I've realised that I haven't remotely done her justice in my narrative, that she doesn't have animated, happy eyes: her lowered, damp eyes are among the saddest I've ever seen. I'm not talking about the eyes of others any more.

No man is a man if he isn't all of humanity – it was you who wrote that. When I first read those words of yours, so true, the raison d'être of almost all literature, I thought that I too could be all of humanity, if I wrote with sincerity and justice. Literature, and that's the chimera, could restore some of the humanity we have lost – don't so many of your books prove that? But justice doesn't exist anywhere, it would seem. All I can feel today is that Preta is all of humanity and she has been detained, she spent three days hungry and thirsty in a dark dungeon, hearing the worst possible insults. That woman would not be a woman if she weren't all of humanity, right? But why aren't we crying with her?

And yet, how strong that woman is, how she believes in the imminence of a new day, in the freedom that is her right, that is the inalienable right of humanity. Eyes can do more than weep, voices can do more than tell stories. Preta sings at the end of the interview, and her singing is beautiful in a way that is hard to put into words. It's a high-pitched voice, a voice that totally floods the room, that spills out from there to cover the whole ruin. And then I once again can see meaning to this effort of mine, not because my writing can have the same potency, it won't do that, condemned as it is to seriousness and paleness. But because it's always necessary to make the attempt – that's what I understand when I look at Preta – even if it's only to fail again, and in that failure, to survive.

Perhaps I'm not very good company right now. I silence these anxieties in time to hear you, to allow your customary humanity to cover the silence I am holding out to you here. In your words perhaps I will be able to find myself, as I have found myself in your pages so many times before.

36.

I wasn't surprised to find her in the hammock, with a book in her hands. That's what her mornings had been like on her days off, waking up early, completing her circuit of the plants and retiring there, escaping from the apartment to occupy a space that was her own, made up of ink and paper and impenetrable thoughts. She seemed to run through the books with a certain eagerness, almost always recent books, almost always written by women, comprising some group whose definition I wouldn't know how to infer. As if there were something she wanted to discover about herself or about the present, as if there were some unsayable question these books might answer. I wasn't surprised to see her that morning, but I thought for the first time that this was her flight, or this was her search, that this was the occupation with which she had been going through the months.

My tiredness was very great but now I didn't want to go to bed, I didn't want to isolate myself in another room that wasn't hers. I dragged my chair over and sat next to the hammock, an arm's length from her skin. For a while we said little, we spread some kind words, and beneath the surface of the words I asked myself what it was, this thing we were living through, if we were alike in that process, and if mourning might perhaps be one way to describe it. Was mourning, ultimately, the most intense experience of disconnection? And why would such a vague feeling, the impalpable loss of something we never had, stretch out for so long? Would it be necessary, as she'd once said, to fill nine whole months, living through the gestation to its end, even if it was the gestating of an absence?

And then my tiredness became greater than any speculative inclination, belittling my customary questionings, or turning them back on myself. Why had I spent so long wanting to hear from her so little, why had I preferred to pay attention only to what others had to say? Did I know this woman so well that I could do without her words, limit myself to deducing her ideas, silencing her without realising it? Would that not be the opposite of intimacy, that being so intimate we find each other predictable, indifferent, and no longer look for each other in the shadow of our own thoughts? Would that not be the greatest gesture of mutual ignorance, two beings becoming infinitely strange to each other, side by side?

Fê, I called out to her, with a timidity even I didn't recognise. Please, don't use my name, it wouldn't be fair, that's not what I'm like, she rebuked me. Can I ask you a question?, I went on. Why did you want to have a child so much, so urgently? She hadn't even started answering and I was already regretting the words I'd chosen, the inappropriate verb tense shutting the attempt in the past, the tone that insinuated it was her fault through an excess of desire. I mean, I tried to correct what I hadn't said, I don't think I ever understood what made you change one conviction for another, so drastically, and become so attached to what you'd spent a decade rejecting.

She closed her book and put it down on the floor: I don't know. She raised her body, gripping the shaky hammock with both hands, and I saw that she intended to think about the matter, that she wouldn't give the ready reply of other occasions. I think I wanted to multiply my feelings, she said at last, my joys and pleasures, my pains and frustrations, I wanted to expand the meanings of life as best I could, you know what I mean. You're going to say, she interrupted me before I could interrupt her, that we were doing that already, and that's why we had work, friends, books, politics, sex. None of that became insufficient, it's true, but I suspect that few novelties could be greater than having that unknown being coming out of my belly and occupying my arms with its urgent needs, with its hunger, its sleep, its distress, its fear, and with its indecipherable laughter, too.

I held out my hand and rested it on her belly, not as if I were touching the child we hadn't had, as if I were touching the child-feeling, perhaps. She went on talking, her gaze lost beyond the window, against a background of motionless trees, motionless buildings, the motionless sky, scouring the motionlessness for a new reply.

I wanted the waiting to be a different waiting. Not to be just that of a body getting old, of friends who no longer see one another, of the country succumbing to torment. I wanted to long for something in the slow passing of the decades. To long for my child's first gestures, for their first night in the bedroom next door, for their new words and the new phrases they'll make out of them, and the unstable tones of their voice until it deepens, and the uncertain features of their face until they become an adult, until the world is more theirs than mine. I think I wanted to give the passing of time a new taste, she said. In the bad times, that's what I feel we've lost, but I know we're not lacking in time, I know a huge future awaits us.

And then I lacked the words to say, but it didn't seem to me that there was anything lacking. I got up from my chair, pulling on the fabric of the hammock, and I found that it opened out wide enough for me to fit inside. I lay in the hammock beside her, now trusting the firmness of the walls. Now trusting the meeting of bodies, she pressed her chest to my chest and made a time another time.

37.

From where I'm writing, I can see the armchair where my father spent his longest hours, I can see the couch on which hundreds of patients revealed their conflicts, revealed their symptoms, tried to convert their dreams, fears, insecurities into words. I cannot imagine what he might have responded to these incessant confessions, an infinity of sentences enclosed within their circumstances, soon forgotten by the patients, long ago dissipated in his own memory. How much of his life was taken up by this continuous dialogue with changeable interlocutors, these infinite words that could leave no mark on the room I am invading now?

It has been quite some time since I arrived here to dismantle his consulting room, when he decided he would move to seeing his patients at home, saving himself the daily effort of travelling back and forth. I was not able to move a single object from its place. Instead I positioned myself at his desk, placed my computer in the centre, spread a few indispensable books around it, started to call the room my study. I write surrounded by his plunder. By his most private library, by sober ornaments and statuettes, by the favela in vertical strokes marked out in an engraving by Renina Katz, by a León Ferrari picture in which two hordes of indistinct little men seemed to be clashing.

This was the place where I wrote the first line, asking myself whether every man was the ruin of a man, where I recounted an episode whose meaning still eludes me today, about a drunk man whose face I can no longer remember. Here was where I described my father's pained arrival at the hospital, and I ask myself why I made that choice. If I wanted to say something about my father, if I wanted to interrogate his identity and yet again to probe his history, why choose to weaken his body and lay him out in critical condition on a hospital trolley? I move away from the desk, I can't stay seated for very long, I lie down on the couch where so many have lain. Why didn't I want to face his enormous past, his trajectory of actions and serious words? Like a belated Oedipus, could I have desired to kill my father and occupy his throne, and support my mother in a now fleshless embrace?

No, I get up and banish these schematic reflections, I've nothing to gain from banal recriminations, from facile regrets. If I remain here even after having finished the telling, even having described in detail everything that did not carry off my father, it is because I have not yet come to understand him, because there is still something I don't know and which insists on summoning me. Where there is a symptom, I'm reading in a passage from Freud that my father has made a point of underlining, there is also an amnesia, a gap in memory. Could this obstinacy of mine about occupying this space be a symptom, and what might the gap in memory be that my words are unable to complete?

I continue to explore his books, I've just spent a few hours reading his articles, clinical case studies, essays. In one of these I discovered an unlikely autobiographical thread, an article in which he talks about the repressed relations between psychoanalysis and politics, and to do this he revisits his own militancy and the various subsequent forms of psychoanalytic action. He asks himself, along with Althusser, about the possibility of an intellectual becoming converted into the masses through an experience of struggle – I can tell from his choice of words that the text is an old one. He himself felt part of the masses, he admits almost embarrassed, he felt a part of the world of the people, and there was something cathartic about that. But he concludes that conversion cannot be quite the right word, there's something religious and mistaken in that idea, it would be much more reasonable to evoke the idea of convergence. It is through affinity that they become close, or rather, one would move towards the other in order to understand its suffering and its power.

His words are serene, almost technical, there's nothing in them that seeks to disturb. I don't understand, then, why my sight turns cloudy and I can no longer read them, I drift away from the text and recover my acute awareness of the space that surrounds me. I cannot find myself in my father's past, in his words and his actions that belong to another time, but I find myself in almost everything he longs for. Would I have wanted to take his dreams, I ask myself back at his desk. Was that why I set out to write about him, to take his place in militancy, in writing, in listening?

I didn't want to kill my father, nor would I have been able to kill him in these pages – my imagination would never have that scope. But I feared his death as though it might contain the inscribing of the end of a whole world, the end of a vision, of a utopia. I feared his death as though it might be my own end – the end that the son I don't have might one day describe. I look up from the page, but I still don't know whether it'll be enough, I don't know if I am capable of leaving just yet.

38.

For a while, I wasn't able to spend time in the occupation. Not that there was anything preventing me, the heavy door with its iron lock hadn't stopped opening, the boy saying welcome had not stopped being there, but no voice was calling me in now and so the meaning of a visit was becoming impossible to discern. Perhaps the call of the moment was a different one, unlike the first, a voice that nobody would ever intone, a voice recommending distance, recommending that I digress from the path I had followed for so many months. As if it were only by losing sight of the occupation that I could make out what I had really seen. As if it were only the contrast with a distant silence that would allow the voices to be heard at last.

And yet, one day, without even knowing what was moving me, without any voice summoning me to go or to stay, I breached the distance with a complete awareness that nothing was being broken. When I arrived at the street, I understood that I didn't want to visit the new occupation, that it was the Cambridge that had attracted me once again. Once I was stationed in the lobby, I knew I needed to climb the stairs one more time, and I was on the third floor when I realised I was already getting out of breath, that my legs were feeling the effects of the lack of exercise. I would keep on going up to the eighth, I decided as though not deciding anything: the reason I had come here was to knock again on Najati's door.

A small gap was enough for me to see his absence. No trace of him could be glimpsed in that room, now crowded with furniture, domestic appliances, rugs, posters, paintings. The family who had taken up residence seemed to greet me with a profusion of smiles displayed in picture frames. No neutral or impersonal detail could remain on view; the accumulation of possessions was their way of stamping their control over the space. Nothing could have jarred more sharply with Najati's sobriety, I saw, with his unwillingness to leave any personal traces, with his refusal to set up a home so far away from the one he'd had to abandon, in a city he could never truly inhabit. Doesn't Najati live here anymore?, I asked as if establishing something obvious, just to relieve the surprise of the person looking at me. The old Syrian guy? He left. Nobody saw him go, he didn't leave any word, nobody knows where he's ended up.

Once the door had closed behind me, I sat down in the windowless corridor, in the gloom that revealed nothing but vague shadows. I was trying to understand the feelings overtaking me, but it was the absence of feeling that seemed to stand out: I wasn't surprised, I wasn't frustrated, I wasn't frightened by Najati's unexplained departure, in no respect did it intrigue me. In the silence of that place, the voice that had now gone quiet was saying something crystal clear. His return to Syria, his return to Homs, now that the inaudible bombing seemed to have stopped, now that in his country there couldn't be a single street corner still left to be destroyed, was logical and necessary. Challenging his official exile, populating the desert of his intimate life with familiar faces. Raising up a new home from the ruins, a solid building on impossible ground, that was the only possible outcome to his story.

In the shadows of that hallway, where there was nobody to see me, I allowed myself to be invaded by improbable images. Najati walking down the streets of Homs without ever stopping at any traffic lights, going past the mosque that had housed his childhood prayers, crossing the garden still sensing the old aroma of the eucalyptus. Najati glimpsing from a distance, beneath a flowering orange-tree, the woman who awaits him with a perpetual wave, her arm still outstretched.

39.

My dear Julián,

Yesterday I remembered the burning sky of my childhood and the ashes falling already cold onto my arms, which were rehearsing a kind of dance in the middle of the smoke. Without a cloud on the horizon, with no birds crossing through the air, the soot was overtaking the landscape. I was convinced that, in some other sky, invisible clouds were being consumed by flames.

The idea of a hidden sky that was devouring itself was very close to the Hell they used to tell me about in Religion & Morality classes. The idea of redemptive angels fighting the flames never occurred to me. That blaze was a forewarning of the Apocalypse. My own internal angels always awoke too late, as if I needed to be subjected to this learning of the end of the world. If that was the lesson, I never learned it. If that was my invitation to resign myself, I would not be so kind as to accept it.

What was happening, in reality, was that, close to our place, they had set fire to the sugar cane fields. The sky that was burning in Mozambique was only, after all, crawling and creeping, prosaic and utilitarian. In recent days ashes have fallen within me that come from a Brazilian sky, from the sky that hangs over the Amazon. Solidarity campaigns have given an account of a world that is aware and available. In some way, however, these voices have reminded us that there is another Brazil, less hyped up in the media, that for months has been devoured by another fire that is blazing through the democracy, institutions and dignity of that great nation.

So I understand your feeling of displacement. I share in that pain as though it were a mourning, a memory of such a recent country that had song and laughter as its flag. You talk about the author's loneliness in the face of his book. Yet I want to talk about that other loneliness that precedes even the author himself, the loneliness that has collectively occupied us all. This lonely condition frightens me because it not only isolates us from one another but also disconnects us from a utopia that grants us somewhere to live in the future.

What is happening in today's Brazil is a great sadness. I know how hard it is to suggest any kind of hope, and that is not what I intend by these lines. Because the sadness of seeing our collective future expiring before our eyes has no name and no dimension. Sometimes, I admit, I do sink into this dejection that has been converted into a deep tiredness. But later, all it takes is a bright morning, the easy laughter of somebody I love, a foolish, free excuse to liberate myself from that dejection. It's that capacity for rebirth that I want to talk to you about.

To write these lines I have returned to one of those places filled with calm and time where we used to sit to talk about stories, characters, and literature. On those days I didn't get the chance to tell you something that I carry with me with the same care with which our ancestors kept a small sliver of fire to ward off the dark and the cold. I was born and lived my first twenty years in a time of fascist dictatorship. My childhood and adolescence were shaped by a cruel regime, one in which fascism and colonialism fed each other. Blacks had a set time when they could move about the city, women lived under house arrest, the poor were only human when they were objects of compassion. My father was arrested by the fascist police, and then tossed into unemployment. Whenever he returned from being questioned, all he would bring back to us was news of the birds he had seen along the way. He never delivered a moan, an insult, any mention of those who humiliated him.

Perhaps this restraint did not require any heroic effort. My father was, in one sense, a privileged man. White, in a colonial nation; a journalist, in an illiterate land; a poet, in a time of ashes. Other people – the great majority – were truly disinherited and the profession they had was always smaller than the race into which they were born. Not once, however, did my father make use of any of those involuntary privileges. The only weapon he drew on for protection was poetry. So powerful was this weapon that it justified him, a peaceful and reserved man, being a cause for fear in those who created fear. And it was just this poetic feeling for the world that gave him the strength, on his return home, to erase the recent humiliation and deliver to us merely his usual awkward smile. And, along with that smile, a made-up account of the birds he had seen along the way.

Dictators in those days were gloomy and unspeaking. They fed off the silence they imposed upon life. Today's dictators are noisy parrots. They talk loudly so they can't hear themselves, and by doing so they can lie again when they need to deny something later. They want to be greater than the regime where they lay their heads.

The fact is this, my dear friend: the world that is born from your books is much greater than the political circumstances surrounding us. Literature ought to assert its own sovereignty and invent birds that, in turn, invent a new sky. And the writer should declare that, even if he is surrounded and threatened, he will travel down paths that are not stained with the moral poverty and the daily imbecility of the rulers of the day. Your book says exactly this in a way that is firm and serene: that literature will remain beyond any occupation. As has happened before, with your *Resistance*.

Mia Couto

40.

Today I remember another burning sky, not from my childhood of serene horizons, but in a much more recent time that was haunted by blazes. It was in the small hours of the morning, I was postponing sleep with indifferent fictions, it wouldn't be long before I would retire to bed, when the dramatic breaking-news chords rang out, in an interruption to regular programming. The first image, which was too close, brought only the fire with its yellow and red locks, the fire blocking out the camera, likewise staining the gentleness of my walls with colour and light. Then right away the image became more distant and the building appeared, split into two halves, one burning intensely, the other subsumed in darkness.

I learned from the alarmed voice of the presenter that it was in the centre of town, and it was a homeless residents' occupation. At that moment they didn't seem to think it relevant to mention the building's address or its name, preferring to highlight the drama of all those non-specific people, those who were running out in despair, those who might still be trapped amid the flames. I was trying to ignore his shrill voice and identify something in the surroundings, something in the façade split between flashes of light and darkness, I was trying to dodge the smoke that was rising, and so arrive at some detail that might appease my fear. I was looking at the powerful light emanating from the windows, I was looking so closely that my eyes were dazzled, and my own reflection was becoming a figure burning in the fire.

I don't know how long I remained trapped in that scene, scouring each discernible body that appeared on the screen before me. I was looking, making no concession to common sense, for Carmen's solid torso, for Preta's strong arms, for Brito's broken leg. I was looking for Rosa, Demetrio, Ginia and so many others of uncertain names. I was most of all looking for the face of Najati, by scant flashes I even found his features in women, in children, the sharp furrows of his skin, his drooping eyelids. By that point I already knew it was not the Cambridge, it wasn't any occupation I was familiar with, it wasn't even a part of the same movement, but that information brought no sense of relief or calm. Consumed by the total disaster, I insisted on watching those unfamiliar faces, no longer to recognise those I had seen before, perhaps to get to know them in that same moment, while there was still time.

And then, in a sudden and incomprehensible thud, consumed by the disaster, that vast concrete body shuddered. It tumbled in mere seconds, as if the ground were summoning it with the greatest urgency, hurling into the air whatever it did not accept, in a dense cloud of embers and dust. And then, born out of that thundery, abject noise, there was silence.

41.

The silence could not be heard when I arrived outside the building, or outside its remains. Helicopters were flying over the scene with their cutting blades, bulldozers were already getting in line to start the clean-up process, men and dogs were turning over rubble in search of remaining life, or of death. The mountain of still-smoking debris seemed to emit a continuous vibration, an incomprehensible buzzing, as if some hidden piece of equipment insisted on decreeing this very obvious end. There was a hubbub emanating from the mass of people on the street, too. Some were crying, others chanting prayers, most speculated on the numbers of the disaster and detailed everything they'd seen since it began.

I don't know how long I spent there, surrendered to paralysis. I know I felt like I was at an uncertain funeral, at a sad ceremony for the death of something vague, incorporeal, something larger than that building or its anonymous victims. To be there was to pay my condolences, it was to share a genuine agony with so many others, but that didn't stop it from also being an obstinate insistence upon suffering, a gesture of morbidness. Pressed against the security cordons, I felt as though this was what

I did every day, tirelessly reading the worst news, greedily consuming the details of the tragedy.

I knew then that I needed to leave that place, to escape from the smoke that was stealing my air, to escape from the repeated laments, from the expressions of dejection. I excused myself dodging past shoulders until the crowd became less dense, until I felt my breath returning to me, my chest filling again. The buzzing was already disappearing behind me, the hubbub likewise becoming inaudible, but still there was no silence – the city was the immensity of its noises.

Buses passed lazily by, following their usual routes, braking with their characteristic squeal. People held out their arms, got on and off, some of them hurried their legs and shouted so as not to be forgotten. One boy gave a loud laugh and he was seen by his mother who was reprimanding him. The city was a constant source of life, making death one contingency among so many, one more of its infinite number of occurrences. In that same minute, and I didn't even need to check, a child was being born in some hidden nook somewhere, adding its cry to the turmoil. Such was the movement of the world, such was the movement of the streets that merely standing still became impossible. It was necessary to keep on going, pacing one's feet to the neighbouring feet, allying oneself to the indistinct mass.

As I turned a corner, the sun blazed full into my eyes, blinding me for a moment. With my eyes closed, I felt as if I was becoming some guy with no origins, with no history, an inhabitant in a single present that is everything even if it lasts nothing, even if it's looking continuously towards the future. That was a bright morning, I realised. And, as I picked up my pace so as not to be run down by the past, I merged at last into the vastness of others.

Acknowledgements

To Najati Tayara, for his moving faith in dialogue.

To Mia Couto, for having made his guidance an act of friendship. To Martine Verguet, Rebecca Irvin and the whole team of the Rolex Mentor and Protégé Arts Initiative, for having made this meeting happen.

To Juliana Caffé, for the transformative invitation to take part in the Cambridge Artistic Residency.

To Carmen Silva Ferreira, Preta Ferreira, and all the welcoming people of the Housing Struggle Movement. I am not dead, I am with you.

To Carolina Motoki, for having lent me Rosa's words. To Demetrio Paiva.

To my dear friends who shared their comments: Tony Monti, Leandro Rodrigues, Abilio Godoy, Tiago Novaes, Roberto Taddei, Fernando Seliprandy, Renato Prelorentzou, Florencia Fuks, Luiz Guilherme Florence.

To Luiz Schwarcz, Julia Bussius and the whole team at Companhia das Letras, for their care, for their efforts.

To my parents, to my siblings, for the unwavering affection and their patience at being transformed into characters.

To Fê, the first reader of everything I write, before I have even written it. For her superlative love, and for the life she has intertwined with mine, so completely.

CHARCO PRESS

Director & Editor: Carolina Orloff
Director: Samuel McDowell

www.charcopress.com

Occupation was published on
90gsm Munken Premium Cream paper.

The text was designed using Bembo 11.5 and ITC Galliard.

Printed in April 2021 by TJ Books
Padstow, Cornwall, PL28 8RW using responsibly
sourced paper and environmentally-friendly adhesive.